Footnote to Doggerel

SHIPWRECKT BOOKS PUBLISHING COMPANY
Rocket Science Press
Winona, Minnesota

Other Books by Tom Driscoll

Bleu (Rocket Science Press, 1997)

Ondine & the Blue Troll, 10 Parables
(Rocket Science Press 2013)

FOOTNOTE TO DOGGEREL

MORE SHORT FICTION

TOM DRISCOLL

Cover and interior design by Shipwreckt Books

Shipwreckt Books Publishing Company
159 Franklin St.
Winona Minnesota 55987

Library of Congress Control Number 2023932830

For Beth—my sweetheart, jardinière, bookworm, pet's pet, and the best damn popcorn maker ever.

FOOTNOTE TO DOGGEREL
Contents

Preface

What we have here is a collection of short fiction spanning forty years of sixty years writing and almost seventy-five years thinking about it. Many of these stories appeared in my 2013 collection, "Ondine & the Blue Troll."

The Africa stories were first written in a wise move to nail down memories of living and working there in the 1980-90s. The title tale, *Footnote to Doggerel*, originally appeared in "The Green Blade," the now silent magazine of the Rural American Writers' Center in Plainview, Minnesota, also defunct since the passing of its founder and sparkplug, Dean Harrington.

Lily Jo is the most recent story, started in 2016, with revisions, cuts, and contemporaneous rewrites in the effort to tease out of clumsy English the almost constant state of mind-altering realism—living with organ failure, no hope of transplant.

1. SAINT MARTIN

Barely keep track of all the voices flowed into Mr. Stanton's curious story. Streams barely seepage crisscrossing unmapped continents only to be pulled by time itself into the turbid river of an old man's long life. Water and stones. Lying there, I became his story. And his mine. The great paradox of a river explored is the ocean at its end, an insatiable belly distended with water and stones. Or so I think, I think. Voices. Water and stones. Nor is the story ever ended. Nor the sea full. Many's One. War & love. Son was Father.

According to Mother, the Old Man used to carry me to work with him in a white wicker bassinette. Lunchtime, she brought me a warm bottle and jars of baby food. Grew up hearing how I learned to walk pushing a shop broom, sweeping puddles of sawdust and oil-dry into a corn scoop held by the Old Man, Red Meacham or one of the other John's Sons mechanics. Before I could talk in sentences, supposedly could name every part of a diesel engine. So little was I the first time I grabbed the spray washer and pulled the trigger on a muddy straight truck—and this I know to be true because I remember it vividly—damn thing blew me clean across the bay into a barrel of solvent.

Remember riding shotgun in John's Sons yellow El Camino. Always chasing parts, making service calls, hiking trucks, going somewhere. Dead of winter, thirty-below, dispatcher'd call the Old Man in the middle of the night. A Binder or Jimmy, Freightliner, KW, Peterbilt, Autocar, whatever, wouldn't start. Couldn't start. Trucks just didn't start in the winter without an engine heater, and even with one, a good, swift boot to the butt, as the Old Man called it, never hurt. He'd drag his sorry ass out of bed, tiptoe into my room, wake me with a shake. Tell me, Get into your skivvies, Charlie-boy. Drag my sleepy ass out of bed. And we'd drive sometimes an hour or longer, enough time for the pickup heater put out some real heat, only to find a sorry ass semi-tractor stranded at a greasy rest stop or a snow packed parking lot waiting for us to give it a shot of go-go juice.

Always was my job to hold the Old Man's flashlight in one hand, can of starting fluid in the other, ready to spray whenever he said, Give her a shot. Smell ether again just thinking about it. Old Man would take apart the air cleaner, connect jumper cables, jack the cab, climb aboard and give that baby a crank. Whatever it took. Ninety-nine times out of a hundred, life rumbled through the frozen diesel. Like a drunk sailor, the Old Man used to say, just got his feets tickled. And every time I'd laugh at the nonsense poetry naturally came out of his small suede mouth.

One winter night, just finishing supper, phone rang out in the other room. The Old Man and Mother always smoked their cigarettes and drank black coffee for dessert. He looked at her, shook his head. Could see he was tired and thinking about letting the phone ring dead. Crushed his cigarette on the plate like he always did, pushed back from the table, got up, went out to the back door and uncradled the old avocado receiver hung there by the basement stairs. Almost hear the man on the other end of the line. "Johnny? Got a tractor won't start. Too damn cold, Johnny. Get it going for me, Johnny?"

Green parka, mittens attached by a cord through the sleeves, landed in my lap. "Won't be long I hope," the Old Man told Mother. Said to me, "Finish your milk."

"Johnny," Mother said sternly. "You be careful. It's late, it's cold, Charlie's got school in the morning."

Other side the river, way out past East Moline on dark factory streets, red brick parapet walls purple with grime, El Camino slewed around a snowplow mountain into an empty parking lot and up alongside a cab-over Freightliner. Like we owned it. Flat windshield, two big sleepy eyes. Old Man groused, driver's probably "rummin' it up" in a gloomy bar scarred with neon rope we passed a couple blocks back. Bumped my door open, jumped out—if I was a fireman. Wind's ascreamin'. Our toes, fingers & noses afreezin'.

Proceeded to fart around must have been close to an hour trying to start that brittle old truck. Diesel just wouldn't pop. Old Man finally gave me the same look he gave Mother at supper. Fed up, she would have called it. Shook his crew cut head—never wore a hat, said they gave him a headache—screwed the cover back over the batteries. Drunken sailor bolted for the service truck, the Old Man's cold feets wrapped in thin white socks that always smelled like an abandoned hayloft when he had me untie the laces and pull off his little black hard soled shoes, crunched across snow, jumped in the El Camino been idling with the heater on high, let out a holler.

First thing always, pushed my lips into frozen fists and blew heat through my mittens to warm my nose and fingers same way the Old Man did his. Then he unzipped his insulated work jacket, matched his dark blue uniform pants, name-of-Johnny stitched over the quilted breast pocket in thick red thread, dug through his heavy white uniform shirt pocket, behind a couple pens and his prized Eversharp, pried out a smoke. Tapped it twice on the horn, digging now in his pants for the lighter. Said out the side his smoky mouth as he flipped his Zippo open and fired up, "Nooo. Wasn't the war scared me, Charlie, half so much as the winter did."

I'm in second or third grade at the time, heard the words war-scared-Charlie-winter, so I responded with childish empathy. "It's really, really cold out."

The Old Man mussed my hair through the parka hood and pom-pom tasseled stocking cap with ear flaps I truly hated but Mother always made me wear. Said, "Keep blowing on those fingers, buster."

Old Man didn't like to have to do service call paperwork in the morning, so we drove back across Twin Bridges and up River Drive past Oscar's and Credit Island and the Garden Addition until we got to John's Sons garage out on the west

5

end of town between Fairmont and Rockingham Road. Entered the shadowy corrugated garage under a wall mounted security lamp wearing a military green shade reminded me of full brimmed steel helmets I'd seen on infantry in pictures from the First World War.

Cold inside, always cold in the garage, just not as cold as outside. Big enough by then the Old Man let me flip on a battery of overhead lights at a breaker panel I could barely reach on tiptoes, faint mud line painted over after the great 65-flood faintly visible at my elbow. Old Man fished three dimes and a fistful of keys on a ring from deep in his pants pocket. Told me go get us each a pop then unlocked a dirty-hand-stained door to his whitewashed plywood office buttressed in winding wooden stairs that led up to parts stored on top. At the pop machine, could see the Old Man through a big glass picture window looked out at the mechanics' bays from a dingy corner of the old scrap iron warehouse he bought in the summer of 1947 after the war. Started his repair shop, fixed beer trucks, stake trucks, dump trucks, delivery vans, semi-tractors, cement mixers, cattle trailers, refers, tankers, piggybacks, lowboys. And commenced to having kids.

Hurried back with an orange for him, cream soda for me. Space heater glowed bright red down on the dark scuffed but everyday swept-up and once a week mopped white linoleum floor. Toasty in the office, Old Man seated at his big grey metal desk, top protected by quarter inch-thick glass he's got pictures of Mother and all his children slid under staring up. Only one of him, standing on a boat dock, middle of summer along the river, one handed hoisting a slimy catfish brown on a butcher hook, must have weighed 75-pounds. Other hand's got an amber beer bottle and a fishing pole twisted through his fingers. Big floppy grin.

So proud of that desk, he was, like a gilded PhD in a gold frame. Desk was a place where only clean digits and perfect penmanship were allowed. The Old Man had small, thick hands, always a little cold too because fact is it's always winter in the truck garage, palms permanently creased with burnt crankcase oil no matter what cleaner he used or how hard he scrubbed them, always sand-papery, cracked and chapped. Before he did anything at his desk, usually took a minute to scrape black gunk from under his fingernails, except the walnut stump stuck out the ring finger, sawed the tip off in high school woodshop, one wicked lick with a sharp handsaw making a wooden knickknack shelf that hung on the living room wall centered over the couch, Mother covered with ceramic angels & the Old Man's model cars & Deborah ended up with.

While he patiently filled out a work order, invoice and timecard for the failed service call, every line and box filled with perfectly legible handwriting, little fussed over curls on all the letters & numbers & checkmarks, I pulled up a chair across from him, knelt on the seat and cleared a space for my Hot Wheels. Liked to play Army with the little metal race cars. They could have fist fights just as easy as they could sprint across the floor, which I wasn't allowed to play on anyway at the garage. Shoot guns, throw grenades, sneak around and attack each other from behind using karate, or team-up, form a stick and parachute like dandelion fuzz behind enemy lines then regroup into a battalion of tanks, or a squad of frogmen wearing wetsuits, had spear guns, knives in their teeth.

The Old Man's desktop was covered with paramilitaristic junk, paper spikes on plywood, pencil holders that looked like antisubmarine mines, assorted engine parts machined from mean looking gunmetal alloys, old pistons, distributer caps, cranks and cams, valves, giant bolts & nuts, armatures, solenoids, springs, things me and my Hot Wheels army might up and decide to attack without warning or perhaps enlist in a battle against one of my favorite targets, a chrome ashtray the size of a Frisbee. Muscle bound Mack Truck bulldog, studded collar, serious under bite, crouched in the middle on stout hind legs, always threatening to pounce off his chrome perch flanked by metal cigar rests that reminded me of jet wings. Nobody dared crush their butts in the Old Man's Mack ashtray though. Didn't even use it for paper clips, pens or loose change. I was the only one allowed to play with it. And believe me, the Mack bulldog was no pussy. He could box better than Ali, and he could fly as long as I didn't bother the Old Man when he's on the phone, or busy thinking.

One Hot Wheels after another crashed into the outer rim of the chrome bulldog bunker and exploded in flames, whose color, heat and deafening roar I simulated with puffed cheeks and quiet rumbling because the Old Man had the desk lamp on, which meant he was working, keep it down. My sounds mimicked everything from small arms fire to atom bombs, guys getting nicked, wacked, massacred, whole platoons wiped out. Incoming Hot Wheels made long, muted whistles punctuated by hushed concussions One after another little cars and trucks tumbled into the bulldog ashtray of doom.

Somewhere in the middle of the Technicolor, stereophonic battle going on in my head, I realized the Old Man was talking. Talking to me. "Sounds like Kraut eighty-eights, Charlie," he said, paused a second then scrunched his eyes shut tight. "Curled up on packed down snow insulating our foxhole, listened to those shells whistle overhead, tried tell if one was gonna land on you."

Johnny Gordon was twenty-six in January 1942 when he enlisted in the Army. That night at the garage, told me he joined-up right after Pearl Harbor to get away from Davenport, see the world. Then spent the next five years dreaming about getting back home. And once he made it back home, spent the rest of his life hoping to see the world again.

A black-and-white photo in the back of a hardcover picture book documenting the exploits of the 28th Infantry in Europe captured a hollow cheeked rifle company buck sergeant wearing shoe polish whiskers, camo net stretched over his helmet. Loved looking at that picture of him spooning beans from a kidney shaped mess kit cup, M1 slung on his shoulder just in case somebody tried to pull any funny business. The Old Man said a Stars and Stripes photographer took that photo during one of many lulls in the battle for the Hürtgen forest, began the fall of 1944. By mid-December, found himself digging a foxhole in another forest, the Ardennes, with the help of a private who'd been rushed to the front to replace one of the twenty-thousand-plus American casualties at Hürtgen.

"Dirt in Luxembourg," the Old Man said, "was harder than tombstone granite."

Roofed their den with thick spruce boughs strong enough to hold a foot of fresh snow fell that first day. Pretty cozy until, middle of the night of the fifteenth, a German eighty-eight sheared the top off a towering spruce standing alongside their location and sent o tannenbaum drilling down like a flaming fighter plane. Impact threw Johnny out the back. Tiny shrapnel from the eighty-eight lodged in his forehead. The Old Man plucked my candy apple red Volkswagen out of the ashtray and dropped it on its nose.

Asked him, "What happened to the other man?"

"Well, Charlie, the other man heard that tree crack and decided he wanted to have a look-see what's going on, just when the bottom of the splintered treetop landed right next to the foxhole. Punched his head through the snow and into frozen ground. Left him deader than a doornail."

"You saw it?"

Old Man looked into my eyes, no expression in his, just winter. "I saw snow covered branches explode like a blue jar full of hand cream." Winked.

"What'd you do?"

"Wasn't much to do, Charlie, except climb back in the hole and wait for Panzerwagens to roll over us. Squad of hungry German infantry come along behind tossing grenades, guns ablazing." How he put it. "Shelled us all night. Tiger Kings came at dawn, then infantry." The Old Man tumbled a Hot Wheels into the bulldog ashtray with a boyish explosion and said, "Find out how bad you want to live when your buddies start getting shot and everybody you counted on to give up their life for you is busy with doing that." Studied his hands a minute. "Was a hard fight, son."

"Did your other friends get hurt?"

"Hurt?"

9

"Like you."

"Wasn't till the next morning, would had to been two days after the Nazi blitz across Belgium started, coast was clear, crawled on my belly foxhole to foxhole looking for anybody might still be alive. Far as I could tell, the whole company— Company-C, son, every one of them a Charlie like you—every one of them was gone."

"Where?"

"Well, either they were dead, or they retreated, or they ran. Decided I better get my tail out of there too. Was that or freeze to death, if I didn't bleed to death first."

He laughed so I laughed. "Did your head hurt very bad?"

"Nah." The Old Man touched the middle of his forehead where an Army surgeon had thirty-years earlier inserted a steel plate to mend the hole left by a sliver from a German artillery shell. "Not too bad. Wrapped a bandage around my head. Looked like a hippie headband your brother David might wear. Stopped the bleeding though. Nah. Hurt a little, but I was too busy worrying about staying warm, keeping my feet, fingers and powder dry to think about the headache."

"I would build a big bonfire. Did you have any matches?"

"Had my Zippo. But I was stranded in enemy territory, Charlie. Couldn't sit around and wait to be rescued. Knew before most the Generals did that Hitler'd punched a hole in our front lines big enough to drive an armored division through. Once they got past Company-C and the rest the dug-in units, a big bulge on the map filled up with Germans. That's why they call it the Battle of the Bulge. Wasn't a hundred-percent sure where I was—somewhere east of Marnach, west of the Rhine River—but as far as I could reckon, I needed to get through the bulge and back over to the right side of the war before winter did me in. I decided the quickest route to the American side would be to follow those German tanks, sneak past them first chance I got, make my way to someplace like Bourcy, or the 101st HQ in Bastogne. What I needed was a pair of snow skis." The Old Man winked like he had a secret.

No secret to me. Knew exactly what snow skis he was talking about. Whole family knew about the Old Man's Nazi snow skis hanging in the shape of an X on the back wall of the garage attached by a breezeway to our house. Parked Mother's Fairlane in there. White metal ski poles, leather wrist straps, dangled down the center between laminated wood skis, dirty white as melted street gutter snow. All the metal parts scaled with rust, ski tips, heavy galvanized bindings, a thin cable tether slipped around your ankle, a wing-nut designed to clip into a toe pin, and a clamp lever stamped with the word Bergans had to pull on to tighten the binding jaw to the sole of your combat boot, way turning a roller skate key pinches the sides of a kid's tennis shoes.

War loot. Brought home an SS dagger too, polished foot-long stainless steel blade in an ebony sheath that my draft dodger brother Mike would one day sell for five-hundred-bucks on Ebay. Couple cut away helmets that eventually disappeared along with the Luger pistol the Old Man took the firing pin of so my brothers could play Army with it.

Old Man stared past me, probably at his own reflection in the office picture window. I used to do that at night when garage bays were dark. Made you look like you're in a monster movie. Said Company-C killed a fair number of Kraut infantry after the tanks busted through their line. Lucky he found one of the dead Germans wearing winter whites, skis and poles hanging in the garage strapped to his rucksack. Quick flashed a man-to-man smile, looked me dead in the eye, which usually meant you were in big trouble and about to get a licking. Smiled and said that Kraut wouldn't be needing skis where he was headed. Jerked up his eyebrows, be sure I knew he meant the Kraut was roasting down in the hot place, which made me laugh.

"Fella with the skis had a little bag of hard wax. Knew enough to rub some on the area right under the bindings. Clamped the steel jaws onto my boot best as I could. Had to cut a hole in both my boots to screw the toes down tight. Wasn't the best thing for my cold feet, but it allowed me to ski southwest into the bulge on Tiger tracks." Old Man let out a triumphant yelp like jumping into a hot service truck. He was happy.

Not sure what to think or say. Almost started bawling. Choked out, "You made it, right?"

"You bet I made it, Charlie. I'm here, aren't I?"

"Good thing you found some snow skis."

"Never ever skied before that day, Charlie. Didn't know for sure if I could even. Just knew I had to." Triumph suddenly drained from his expression. Gave me a look so despairing, really did cry to myself for a second. Said, before trying on the skis, he collected food, water, ammo and dog tags from dead soldiers. But in all the confusion, forgot about the Private who lost his head. Left his tags behind. "Knew him barely a week, forgot him overnight."

The Old Man picked up an open pocketknife he used to open mail and for fingernail cleaning, reached out and adjusted the long, wiry neck of his desk lamp, eased the blade into his thumbprint and dug so deep for a splinter he drew blood. Squeezed the incision, finger tweezed out a black metal barb the size of a typewriter hyphen, studied it a second, showed it to me on the tip of his pinkie. "Off that Freightliner," he said. "So cold, never felt it." Rubbed the splinter invisible the way a magician makes a bird disappear.

Pulled my Hot Wheels limited edition cement mixer out of the ashtray. One of my favorites, it could cream any of the regular cars in fair fight. Plus, I loved the big ready-mix trucks came in John's Sons to get worked on. Glided it across the glass desktop into the Old Man's hand. I knew what dog tags were. My brother David gave me one of his when he got home from Okinawa. Asked the Old Man, "Did you get in trouble for not taking the private's dog tags?"

Laughed, "No." Sproinged the mixer back to me like a marble. "In all the confusion that day, my first job was to stay alive. That meant learning how to ski before the sun went down. Must looked like your mother's old treadle sewing machine, slipping along, poles holding me up as much as pushing me. Skied till dark. Stopped, then scooped myself a little cocoon out of the snow and tried to sleep. Pretty quick realized though, if I fell asleep in my sweaty clothes, I'd freeze for sure. Couldn't risk a fire to warm up, dry out, didn't know where the Krauts were. I got up, ate a chocolate bar, smoked a cigarette, jumped back on the track." Old Man chugged his arms like a train. "Skied all night and most the next day. Had those skis barking like dogs once I got the hang of it."

"Did you fall down ever?"

Tapped himself out a smoke, lit it, smiled again. "Lost count how many spills I took. Lucky I didn't break something." Burped a chuckle. "Never did master skiing down hills, even little ones, be a turn at the bottom." Slapped the desk. "Down I'd go. Some pretty rough terrain. Those tanks knocked trees over, kicked up boulders, ice, grass, mud. Had to cross railroad tracks, highways and ditches. No choice sometimes but take the skis off, which was chore in itself, and walk, which was slow and cold. Didn't break any speed records. Figure by afternoon of the second day, made it back across the Belgian border. Covered maybe twenty miles."

"Then were you safe?"

"Not quite yet. Even if I got past the Krauts and made it to an Allied camp, nobody was safe until the Germans were stopped. And far as I could see, the Germans were just getting started. Came to a steep bluff overlooking a wide valley. Must have been a couple hundred armored units spread out maybe two miles away from where I stood, Panzer Kings, Panthers, heavily armed halftracks towing antitank guns. Appeared to be refueling. Troops taking a little break before the next push west. Then out of nowhere, heard a voice. About jumped out of my skin. Man said, 'O river.'"

"Was he a Kraut?"

"Couldn't tell. Sounded out of breath, like he'd been chasing me. I turned real slow, trigger finger hooked in the .45 I took off Lieutenant Harper. 'Looks like it starts in that there marsh,' he said. 'Not the Meuse. Could may be the Ourthe.' Southern accent belonged to a tall, clean shaved G.I. didn't look the worse for wear. Got an OG blanket draped over one shoulder like a bullfighter. He's scanning the distance with a pair of Nazi field glasses. Private stripes. Riding a pair of German skis looked just like mine. Took me a couple heartbeats, but when it sank in I was looking at another American, one who's breathing, felt so happy, would have kissed him right there except he pointed northwest into thick woods. 'Little bridge up there a piece, Sarge. You see it? Five'll get you ten, that's where the Krauts cross. Not as fast as fording the swamp, but a lot safer. Objective is to make to the other side. Bourcy and Noville dead ahead. Krauts take Noville, kiss goodbye to Bastogne.' He lowered the glasses, looked at me, 'What would you do, Sarge?' Told him generals are paid to think. I'm paid not to. We both had a good laugh over that. I shook out two cigarettes. Told him the tanks we're looking at down the valley overran my unit. Figured he had to probably been with Company K, dug in a mile or so south of Company C, end up on skis same time and place as me, or Bravo north of Charlie. Asked him if Kilo got hit hard. Private tossed his chin all the way back east. 'Ever-body's dead.' Reminded him, 'Everybody's dead but me and you.' That's when we really sized each other up. Can't be too careful, Krauts all over the place. He looked me right in the eye, pulled a knot of dog tags out the pocket of his fatigue pants, said, 'Possible one or two others got out alive. No morn that. You could say we was hit hard. Looks like you got hit pretty hard yourself, Sarge. Why'nt let me have a look under that bandage? Fix you up with a clean one.'"

"Was he a medic?"

"Medics in those days had a big white cross painted on their helmets. Didn't see one on his. Told me he was a radioman. Asked him where the radio was. Said it was ruined. Saved his life, took a bullet for him. Said, 'Let me change that bandage. Guarantee make you feel better, Sarge.' Both of us stood there leaning on ski poles while he patched me up. One thing for sure, little canteen water, little iodine, clean belly wound compress and a new bandage tied not too tight, felt like a new man. When he was done, asked him his name. Said he was St. Martin."

Almost spilled my pop when I heard that, little Catholic brat drilled in catechism by the nuns at St. Alphonsus. "Saint Martin? He was a real saint? Did he have a halo and everything?"

"Not that kind of saint, Charlie. No halo, no wings, just a pair of dog tags hanging inside a private's uniform with the name Martin St. Martin stamped on them. Didn't have time to ask where he's from. Germans had been being quiet, when machinegun fire cracked the silence like a broke bat double. Private St. Martin raised his binoculars and scanned the river valley. Lifted the leather strap and pointed as he handed the glasses to me. Down on our south flank, a squad of Krauts the size of ants in the snow hounded what looked to be an American soldier judging by his green coat. No helmet on, no hat even, no weapon. He's running for his life in knee deep snow over marsh grass, ice and frozen muck. Got a quarter mile head start at the most. Krauts don't seem in a hurry. They're taking turns taking potshots. Didn't really stop to think, just said that the poor guy needs help. No sooner did I spit out my cig, St. Martin's skiing downhill through heavy timber across the west face of that bluff. For a southern fella with an Ozark twang, St. Martin sure could schuss. Broke trail for me all the way to the bottom and across frozen swamp. Returned the favor by not busting my leg, leave him in the lurch. Skied right up behind the Krauts. They're too busy lobbing wide shots at their turkey to notice us prone in the snow. I pointed out my four Kraut targets to St. Martin. St. Martin nodded, pointed to his four. And we attacked. Pop-pop-pop-pop. Son's a guns didn't know what hit 'em, Charlie. Eight Krauts down. No movement in our direction from the main force. They're too busy queuing up to cross the narrow bridge."

"What happened to the turkey man?"

"Saved him. Turned out to be Duncan Riley from Company C, my outfit. Half froze. Scared out of his wits. St. Martin pulled the blanket off his shoulder, unsheathed a bayonet and slit the blanket in two. Wrapped half around Riley's neck with a pat on the back, folded the other half, draped it back over his left shoulder.

"That was nice of him."

"Sure was. No time to get too cozy though, Kraut patrol missing. Caught our wind and duck walked, skis and all, across the swamp. Other side, we crouched in tall red reeds bent by snow drifts, took the first long rest in a long time. St. Martin opened a ration for Riley, but Riley was too shell shocked to eat. Hated to do it but threaten to shoot him myself if he didn't simmer down, stop babbling about deserting his post when the Kraut infantry rushed our foxholes after eighty-eights and Panzers flattened them. Felt bad for Riley. Ardennes Forest was his first fight. But wailing like that, get us killed. Pulled the .45 and told him to shut his trap. Damn deserter."

Never before had I heard the Old Man swear. I mean, I heard swearing. At my age, in my school, saying damn was just as obscene as saying shit or fuck, all words I more or less understood. Shit was a turd, what Mother called a job. Fuck meant very ugly or very mad. And damn was the same as calling somebody a devil. But I never heard the Old Man swear. Made me feel worse to hear him say damn deserter like that. Asked sweet as any little Catholic boy could be for clarification, "Dad, is a deserter a yellow belly like Mike?"

The Old Man drained his Crush, stuck two fingers down the necks of our empties, clinked them into a wooden pop case he kept next to the waste basket, puzzled look on his face, asked me, "Where did you hear Mike is a yellow belly?"

"I don't know."

"Because it took a lot of courage for Mike to do what he did. Stuck to his guns, went to Canada rather than fight a war he believed deep in his heart was wrong. Gave up everything. Don't agree with what he did, but he's not a yellow belly. Neither was Riley. He ran from the battle, and that's wrong, but he had shell shock. Know what shell shock is?"

"What?"

"Remember I told you about the eighty-eights whistling overhead before they crashed into our foxholes?"

"Yes."

"Well, Charlie, sooner or later, after those shells land on foxholes all around, coming closer and closer to you, you get shell shock. Only two things you can think of, curling up in a ball and escaping."

"Were you and St. Martin deserters, you escaped?"

"I escaped, Charlie, but I didn't desert. Never crossed my mind to. But then, I didn't get shell shock. I got a Bronze Star."

"You did?" No idea what a Bronze Star was, but I knew stars were good. "Geeze. Did you get a medal?"

"Bronze Star is a medal. Got a Purple Heart too, and a V-pin for Valor, and a Special Commendation Medal."

"That's a lot. What's a special communication metal?"

"Commendation Medal. I got that for something I did later, after I made it back to the rear."

"Were you safe then?"

"Eventually I was safe. Took a little while. Once Riley calmed down and me and St. Martin had a chance to think a minute, we moved out to the southwest hoping to find a road not swarming with Krauts. Pretty soon, came to a round point where two hard roads intersected, one north-south, the other east-west crossed by railroad tracks. Milepost said we were nine kilometers north of Bastogne, two-k east of Bourcy, five from Noville. Didn't take a logiOisín to know that there were Krauts all around us, some probably headed our way. St. Martin said there was a seventy-five percent chance the armor we saw crossing the bridge would turn south and intercept us at the intersection where we stood. Didn't have time to ask how he figured that out. Little bird told me he was probably right though. Riley started to fuss again. St. Martin, as if he needed a guide, asked me which way should we go. I looked over at a small brick building next to the tracks, gravel apron leading out to the road. Asked St. Martin if he knew what it was for. Private's face lit up. Said he thought it was a telephone relay station. Saw a light bulb go off over his head as he studied the lines coming in one side, going out the other. Didn't have to say anything. Grabbed Riley and followed St. Martin inside. Found blood on the floor, an American helmet I plopped on Riley's head. Electronic equipment either smashed or sabotaged, wires ripped out, tubes shattered. St. Martin went to work removing a panel covered with plugs. No more than ten minutes went by, he spliced in a headset with alligator clips, pushed and pulled jacks for a while, then muttered a few words. Handed the headset to me. Said it was Twentieth Armored Infantry headquarters. Captain Bendix. Told him who I was, Sergeant Johnny Gordon, where we were. Told him about the Kraut armor crossing the little river, couple hundred tanks, refueled, ready to fight. Support infantry. Captain Bendix talked to another officer, addressed him Major, Sir. Finally got back on the horn and told me to get out of there. Head due west. Stay to the south of Bourcy. They were already taking fire. Past Bourcy, only a couple miles northwest to Noville. He said, 'Sergeant, keep ahead of those tanks because they're probably coming this way. Some may shoot down to Bastogne. Be a big help if you keep an eye on their movement, report which way they go. But don't slow down for long.' Told him we had field glasses and skis. Then he said, 'One more thing, Johnny.' He said, 'Don't get captured.' Said a report came in that very morning. Krauts massacred a hundred, hundred-fifty American prisoners day before up in Malmedy." Old Man looked at that picture of himself holding a catfish. Rubbed both hands though his thinning brush of hair, almost white as I recollect. Looked at me, his round face a wrinkled rubber mask, lopsided, grinning. "Boy, we hightailed it outta there."

"You made it though. Right?" Rolled my canary yellow Camaro across the desktop, hit him in the elbow where dark grease permanently stained his shirtsleeve.

He walked stick fingers up to the car, made clicking sounds like opening the door. Got in and fired up a dragster. Revved the engine a couple times using the muffler of his throat, popped a wheelie, peeled out and sent the Hot Wheels back across the desk glass to me. Then answered my question, "Not so fast, buster. Had to get Noville, good three miles. While I was talking to Captain Bendix, St. Martin went outside, stood watch on a foot patrol across the swamp. They discovered the dead Krauts been shooting at Riley. We left a clear trail, and they were headed in our direction. If that weren't bad enough, you could hear the chatter of tanks in the distance, couldn't see them though yet."

Movie playing in my head, and I'm in it, gunning and shooting like we played at recess, bullets whizzing all around, getting hit, knocked down, roll in a cloud of dust, jump back up, take out a tank with a grenade, spit out another pin, take out another tank. "What'd you do?"

"Backpacked our skis and ran like the wind, Charlie, straight down the middle of the highway until I figured we had enough of a lead, we could risk leaving tracks in the snow again and beat a path for the woods. Skirted south of Bourcy. Sounded quiet, but Captain Bendix said do not get captured, so we kept going. Krauts never caught up with us. Made it to a roadblock east of Noville on Bourcy Road by late afternoon. Turning warm, foggy. An infantryman ushered us to headquarters in the center of town. Reported what I knew to Captain Bendix. We're here, Germans aren't far behind. Captain lifted up my helmet, saw the blood-stained bandage. Ordered me to have a medic look at the wound. Turned to PFC Riley, he's wrapped in the half blanket St. Martin gave him, cowering. Captain asks Riley if he's ready to fight. Riley said, 'No sir.' Said, 'Please, I can't.' Started bawling. Captain looked mad as the dickens but ordered the Infantryman to escort me and Riley to a field hospital. Ordered St. Martin to a machinegun emplacement on the north road out of town."

Shelling and shooting started around four in the morning. I'm lying on my back on a cot. Had me good and doped up. But I knew the minute the real battle began a few hours later. Wasn't like I could sleep, fighting and all, but wasn't like I could jump up off that cot and defend myself either if Krauts rushed the hospital. Knew Riley wouldn't. Worst feeling, feeling helpless as an old grandma. Next thing I remember, somebody's waking me up. Everything's real quiet. In the calm, a couple medics put me on a stretcher, shoved me in the back of a duce with a bunch of other wounded soldiers, a lot lying on stretchers, the rest crammed onto bench seats. There's Riley, still got St. Martin's blanket wrapped around him, still cowering. Drove us south to a village called Foy, about halfway between Noville and Bastogne. All the while we're traveling south, listen to the sound of heavy traffic headed north, reinforcements and ammunition for the boys holding Noville."

"Did the boys beat the Krauts?"

"Stopped them in their tracks, Charlie," the Old Man laughed. "Lost a lot of good men that fight, got knocked backwards a few times, but the enemy lost a lot of men too. Ran out of ammo. Ran out of fuel. Ran out of luck. Our boys eventually whipped the Krauts, sent them back to Berlin with their tails between their legs."

"Did St. Martin make it?"

"St. Martin? Yeah, he made it. Ended up in Bastogne for a few days. Me and Riley ended up there too."

"Did Riley get better from shell shock?"

"Riley went to the stockade, Charlie. Jail."

"But he had shell shock."

"I know. A lot of soldiers had shell shock. A lot of them didn't abandon their post though, or if they did, they didn't disobey a direct order to go back to their post like Riley did."

"What happened to Riley?"

Old Man lit another cigarette. "Riley was facing a court martial for desertion, maybe a firing squad. He wasn't alone. Stockades were full of deserters refused to fight any more. Dozens of investigations going on. Army was looking at everybody who wasn't out there chasing the Krauts."

"Even you?"

"Even me. St. Martin. Riley. One day, an officer came to see me in the hospital while I was waiting to be shipped further to the rear, get this steel plate put in my head. Told me Riley'd told him I fought hard in the foxhole at Marnach, killed a few Krauts that first day of the battle, few more at the river when me and St. Martin saved him. St. Martin told the officer none of us would have made it to Noville, hadn't been for me. Army wanted to give me a medal. Army also wanted to know more about St. Martin."

"Did St. Martin get a star too?"

"No, Charlie. St. Martin didn't get any medals."

"How come? He was a good shooter, I think. Did he get shell shock chasing Krauts to Berlin?"

"Charlie, St. Martin was a German officer."

"A Kraut?"

"A Nazi Kraut."

Didn't want to believe what I was hearing. In my mind movie, St. Martin played an American hero, not a yellow-bellied Kraut. "But, daddy, St. Martin helped save you."

"Yes, he did. But he was a Nazi officer, a deserter. And his name was not St. Martin. I suspected as much when we met."

"How'd you know?"

"The rifleman who died in my foxhole when he looked out and the tree hit him in the head? I forgot to take his dog tags off? His name was St. Martin too. Private Martin St. Martin."

Felt bad as I ever had all of a sudden, the heroic image of Saint Martin bandaging Sergeant Johnny Gordon in the war of the bulge tarnished. "What was his name? The Kraut?"

"Kolonel Werner Krause. He was an engineer who'd been stationed most of the war in Poland. Because he'd studied I guess in America and spoke English so well, Germans sent him behind American lines a week or so before the Battle of the Bulge started. His job was to disrupt communications, cut phone wires, destroy relay stations, point road signs the wrong direction, anything to confuse the Allies in Belgium."

"Did Krause get the firing squad like Riley?"

"No, Charlie. Neither one of them got the firing squad. Major Stanton told me Riley finally agreed to go back to a combat unit. Last I heard, he disappeared again, never heard from since. The Major took charge of Kolonel Krause. Questioned him for a month, then sent him to a war prisoner camp in Iowa. Told me Krause would atone for his mistakes. Think Stanton liked him."

"This Iowa?"

"This Iowa. Algona, up on Minnesota border, there was a big camp for German prisoners."

"Still?"

"Algona is still there. The camp is long gone. The war is over, Charlie." Old Man reached across the desk, pulled me by my head and kissed me on the hair. Smelled his cigarettes and supper coffee. "Only battle left is winter," he said. "Better pack up your Hot Wheels, buster. Get you home before Mother worries herself sick thinking I took you to see the Irish play again."

Mother. She never forgave the Old Man for the time he took me along when Red Meacham delivered a repaired Freightliner to Des Plaines then we all rode to South Bend in the El Camino to watch the Boilermakers whip Notre Dame and Red and the Old Man drank so much whiskey Red practically tore off some poor saps head for dinging the El Camino bumper in the parking lot and me and Old Man had to spend the night in the camper at a truck stop while Red spent the night in jail. O, Mother war pist.

  & Mother war a WAC,

  & parachutes she packed,

  & deuced a Jimmie once

  & a half oops, smacked a Jeep

  & wracked her bumpers

  & the Old Man wd say,

  & I looked up't driver'd smack't me

  & thought twar a angel a saw

  & asked her 2 back up & 2 merry ma.

Real truth is, Mother got out the WACs in '45, swapped her fatigues for a leather apron on an assembly line at the Harvester plant in Rock Island. Would tell me in the wake of the Old Man's passage, they met at the Vet's on New Year's Eve. Looking for a good man looking for an honest woman to settle down with.

Sometime after midnight, half-snockered civilian named Johnny, come lately back from post-war Germany, winked her to join him at a bar on Harrison Street by the overpass where the train depot sat in those days. There they drank Jack Daniels raw, listened to an old Negro piano player lived in the Davenport ghetto buried on the hill above the switchyard. Between passing trains, boogie-woogied their reds, whites & blues till the sun came up.

Happy couple went out on that first day of 1947, having tentatively decided time had come to hit the hay, but twas so cold the Old Man's 1935 two door, five window Ford coupe wouldn't turn over. Within six months however did they become man & wife. Sister Deborah pushed out the following spring and John's Sons war born.

Was my older sister Deborah drove Mother up from Iowa to visit me on a bleak late winter day shortly after the V.A. docs released me into the custody of Boxcar Taylor, who gave me a lift back to the empty lake cabin we called the Outhouse, which is where my better half Geneva had parked my car before bailing on me. Remember Deborah carried a paper plate full of cookies, fat with chocolate chips judging by the smell leaked out crimped aluminum foil. "Made you some treats, Char." The only Gordon girl, Deborah, fifteen-years my senior, stared disdainfully at the painted Cataract I broke with my fist and patched with a dirty plywood scrap I filched from the neighbor's woodpile. Asked, "Want one?"

Shook No my head. Never did develop a taste for Deborah's cooking. Been Mother's chocolate chips, probably have let one melt in my mouth. Old Man always smiled at her and said as though he was first to think of it, Quickest way to a man's heart's through his stomach, Mother.

Never forget, when I was in basic training, Mother, sharpshooting for the heart, mailed me a birthday cake. Arrived totally smashed, totally delicious. Shared it over beer in the dayroom with my basic buddies, nun slapping each other's hands be the one to scoop out the last of the icing off the pizza flavored cardboard disc she shipped it to me on.

Mother didn't stop cooking until she stopped driving, age-eighty, when Deborah decided it was time to pull the plug on car accidents and stove fires waiting to happen. Sold Mother's ancient Fairlane and the house I grew up in, moved her to an apartment with only a microwave. Bathroom big enough land a 747 in. Missed Mother's cooking the worst way that overcast day at the Outhouse, melting snow, the lake a rumple of dirty toilet paper. Missed ma. She was nothing like the Old Man, but he completed her. Gave her something none of us kids even really knew existed until it went to the grave with him.

Soon as she walked through the Outhouse door, noticed her cough, first sign of a heart problem that would kill her early in the morning on Valentine's Day when she was eighty-six. Couldn't have helped her heart any standing there wearing a cheap blue polyester pantsuit, looking at the spitting image of her long late husband, head still wrapped like rump from the locker she always fixed on Sundays. Old Man's all-time favorite.

Mother eased herself down on the foot of my bed near the simmering woodstove. "I'm sorry I couldn't come to see you in the hospital," she said.

Deborah jumped in. "Muth had a bad cold. I didn't want her exposing everybody at the Medical Center to that."

Asked Mother, "Feeling better now?"

"Just old, Charlie. I feel fine. Not in any pain."

"That's good."

"What about you?" Waved a shaky hand. "Does your head still hurt?"

"Don't even notice it, Mother, except when I go to comb my hair in the mirror."

"Your eyes look clear. You look good."

"Nothing hurts, eyes aren't clouds, I'm good. Going back to the academy. Everything's good."

Mother mentioned Deborah called the V.A. every day while I was there. "Your doctor told Deb he doesn't know for sure if it's delayed stress disease or it something else." Mother's voice sounded worn out from smoking pretty much non-stop since she joined the WACs and got a taste of the Pall Malls. Eyes runny with uncertainty. She looked at her knees. Said to Deborah, "I don't know."

"Muth, it's PTSD," whispered Deborah, reserving a condescending glance for me. Don't mean to imply that Deborah was any kind of monster. She wasn't. Or that she didn't love me, Mother, or the Old Man, because she did, and I knew she did. Brother David called her a slut when she got pregnant, had to marry Lester, so she didn't much love David. And Mike, she hated Mike for going to Canada. Didn't understand why anybody wouldn't jump at a chance to become a general, boss people around, maybe plug a few full of lead as a lesson to the rest. But like the Old Man said to me once in strictest confidence, Deborah just was born pushy. And she loved me. "It's a syndrome," she corrected Mother, "not a disease. For goodness sake, Charlie's not crazy."

"Well thanks for that, Deb," I slathered a half assed laugh in sarcasm. "Got a little shell shock going on is all. Right Mother?"

Mother's dentures went slack, a sure sign she was trying not to laugh. Mumbled through a handful of dice, "I know they don't call it shell shock anymore," before a titter turned into a coughing fit. Life leaked out her, vapors of sadness, shame maybe. Darkness for sure, little bitter coldness. To this day, I blame it on the doublewide oxblood granite headstone she bought when the Old Man kicked. Names & dates, everything but the year of her highly anticipated termination neatly carved in stone as they say, a deadweight on an invisible ankle chain dragging her into the plot. Stopped driving, quit cooking, exhaled life while hanging onto a stainless-steel grab bar in her sit down shower after shitting herself. Hell of an end to her story. Couldn't say anything made sense half the time, just pitiful noises, painful sighs can't be spelled.

Finally, Deborah said, "So is, what's her name—Geneva? She's gone then?"

Didn't appreciate being made to feel like a baby brother & a big loser, so I didn't answer. To begin with, Mother's the only one in the family ever met Geneva. We drove down to Davenport one Saturday, took Mother out to eat at Reife's, her favorite spot forever used to be up on Locust near 5-Points. Deborah worked as a carhop there in high school before the drive-in part closed. Mother had on a clean diaper, but still smelled up the restaurant bad once she peed it full. Geneva wheeled her chair into the bathroom. Came back jabbering like best friends. Mother ordered a tenderloin. Took one bite, squirted ketchup all down her cheek, started laughing, then coughing, then crying. Waitress put the sandwich in a doggie bag along with a handful of hard candy for her to take home. On the way back to the assisted living high rise down by the old Sears store, Mother patted my leg, looked into the cramped back seat where Geneva sat, wound up and stammered for probably ten-seconds, "Iyyye liiiiike herrrr."

"Anyway," continued Deborah, pacing between the Cataracts and the front door like a dog's got to go, "best that you and Geneva have gone your separate ways. I'm not blaming her. You just weren't ready yet."

"Ready for what yet, Deb?"

Deborah pointed the heel of her hand at me like she's casting a spell. "I remember daddy is all."

"What?"

"You know what, Charlie. Daddy was wounded in the head too, and never got over it."

"Yes he did."

"No he didn't. And you'll never get over him."

"Deb, please. I can't do this right now."

"Do what?"

"Talk about the Old Man. Let's talk about something else."

"I don't like it when you call him that. He was your father."

"Jesus Christ, Deb. Jesus Christ. Can you give it a rest?"

Mother struggled to produce the dirty look for my sister she had perfected when Deborah was a teenager. Took her a while but nailed it. Sourpuss she called it. Then, slow, slurring, she said, "Deborah, stop pestering your brother. Your father isn't here anymore."

Wish I could say the Old Man keeled over on a service call while I was standing there shivering my ass off beside him holding the ether can, but that's not what happened. Fall of 1982, the Old Man's doc diagnosed him with pancreatic cancer. Kept the bad news to himself for a month, then, "according to Deborah," he asked her for a five-thousand-dollar loan so he could go back to Europe before he died. Deborah, who had become the richest member of the family by selling real estate, gave him the money but didn't tell anybody about the Old Man's plan, including me, including Mother.

Couple days after he went missing, Deborah cracked like a rotten egg, confessed the Old Man was dying of cancer, ran off to the Battle of the Bulge. Said he made her swear on a stack of Bibles not to tell a soul. Few days after that, the Old Man called Mother from a hotel room in Noville, Belgium. She blubbered so hard the whole time, snot and tears slimed up her words. Shook her fist at God, yelled at the Old Man, "You did what you had to, Johnny, I understand that. You had friends die there, you had to say good-bye to them. But now it's time for you to get home. You hear me? Get home! You need to see a doctor, and Charlie needs to see you."

The Old Man headed back. Got as far as Union Station in Chicago and keeled over, dead as a doornail. Blame it on the train. He loved trains more than he loved trucks. When I was five or six, up from the basement he hauled a big box filled with HO track, transformers, locomotives, cabooses and freight cars, trestles, houses, a depot, bank and school, streetlights, crossing gates, the whole HO world down to little trees, shrubs, school kids and policemen. Told me he packed all of it up, put it away when David and Mike got too old play with it nice, started crashing the trains into model cars and using the HO people as civilians for their Army men to attack. Was my turn to play with it, he said, before I turned too old too.

Train took over the dining room table for a month of Sundays. When we weren't at the garage, we played with the trains. And when he died, Mother told everybody, "Johnny loved trains so much, took one to see God."

When my oldest brother David arrived home with the Old Man's casket, Deborah's story changed. Her and Lester it turns out had traded fifteen-grand for John's Sons. John's Sons would become Deb-Les Transport & Development. Deborah got the business and Mother got an extra thirteen grand in the bank.

After the Old Man died, Mother kept me out of school from just before Christmas until the first week of February. Might never have gone to school again except Deborah kept telling Mother, "He can't stay home forever." Day I started back in Sister Carissa's class, remember wet snow at recess, sky the color of vomit. All the boys retreated to one corner of the playground to pack fat snowballs to throw at the girls. I just stood around feeling dead. Then I heard this one kid named Jason yell, "Gordon is it!" Lobbed a softball, exploded on my chest like a rotten orange. Couple other kids pitched at me too, but I dodged. Took cover behind the steps went up the slide and started quick packing grenades. Slide's getting pelted, whack-whack-whack. Soon as I had an armful of deadly ammo, I jumped up and attacked. Smacked Jason in the head, knocked his hat off. He dropped to his knees and started bawling. I blasted him some more. The advantage suddenly mine, bunch of kids deserted Jason, ran over and covered me at the slide while I reloaded and fired again. Eventually, the recess bell rang, ending the battle of the balls. Everybody except me returned to class for geography. I walked home, but didn't go in the house, didn't want Mother to know I was back. Went in the garage. Took the Old Man's Nazi skis and poles off the wall, snuck down to Highway 61 across from John's Sons. Deborah hadn't yet had time to change the sign out front.

Far west end of Davenport back then, nothing much between River Drive and the Mississippi but a marshy floodplain dotted with concrete manholes connected to a maze of future industrial park storm sewers everybody's parents warned their kids not to play in. I clamped on the heavy battle skis, screwed their rusty wing nuts over my toes, slipped my hands high into the pole straps and broke trail south through a blowing snowstorm that made me feel like I was chasing the freezing exhaust of Kraut Tiger Kings. Despite my size, I made good progress. When I got to the new interstate bridge, its center arch painted blue or yellow, I forget now, I decided to ski on across the river, get as far away as my imagination would take me.

Slow going in deep, slushy snow. Impossible to determine the quality of the ice underneath. Not that I was thinking about what supported me. Wasn't thinking much of anything as I recall. My focus, completely, on skiing to a place only I knew how to find, if it could be found, a place where I would reconnect with the Old Man. I was mad as the dickens at him. But I was convinced, beyond any rational thought, because I knew what I was doing was childish & crazy, that if I found him, he would be so happy to see me, he'd kiss me. I was Saint Martin. I would clean his wounds and tear my blanket in two, half for me, half for him, and this time he would not allow Major Stanton to send me to prison for stealing a headless private's dog tags. I was the good Nazi. I was twelve years old, and a half.

Skied out onto the main channel, which commercial pushers would begin moving coal and grain barges through within a matter of weeks. Promptly fell right into a narrow crack in the ice, left my arms and poles splayed across the snowy surface, my chin resting on the river's belly, the rest of me submerged in its unforgiving depths.

Drivers approaching that interstate bridge from Iowa descended a tall bluff as I recall, a sharp-eyed hawk gliding down into the Mississippi Valley. Trucker who'd been watching me ski toward the bridge thinking I was maybe a deer, saw me fall through the ice. He called the Illinois Highway Patrol on his CB radio. Spent about half-an-hour in the water. That's what I was told, anyway. Lucky to be alive, everybody said the way you chasten a fool boy with a positive message. Wasn't exactly unconscious when they rescued me but wasn't aware of rescuers pushing a fireman prone on an extension ladder out across thin ice to get me. I was in a parallel universe for the first time. Was with the Old Man.

First, I didn't recognize him because I'd already forgotten what he looked like. But he recognized me. Kissed me on the top my head. Then I really saw his face, the black & white one in the back of the 28th Infantry book. He had a hole in his head you could see daylight through. He had a halo too. And wings. We were in heaven together. It was nice there. Blue sky. Not cold. Like summer, forever.

Rescuers had to take off my shoes to fish me from the drink, let them sink. Skis and all disappeared.

Opened my eyes. There in my hospital room is Mother, Deborah, her husband Lester and Red Meacham in a dirty blue John's Sons uniform, all smiling at me like I was puppy they're thinking of taking home. When I opened my eyes again, everybody except Mother is gone. "I can't stand seeing you in a hospital," she said. "Don't you ever scare me like this again, Charlie! What were you thinking?"

Looked at her, still confused. Remember saying, "Twas a angel a saw," just like the Old Man used to.

Shook her fist at God. Pointed her finger at me, eyes full of vinegar, blubbered, "Charlie, you are not your father."

Mad at Mother, mad at the Old Man, boy o boy mad at everybody. Jimmied hisself up on one elbow, I did, rose out that hospital bed, red stained bandage covering the daylight in his head, twar me I mean, and bleated at a angel o death with pubescent colic, "Never claimed be my father, muth!"

2. NZOMBI

Mid-September 1991, Laurence Langdon, Political Officer at the American Embassy in Kinshasa, Zaire, discovered a Classified monograph among archives secured by U.S. Marines during a bloody mutiny by unpaid Zairian soldiers against Mobutu Sese Seko, dictator at the time, the leopard man, Ngoi.

```
        The Truthful Account of
   How I Was Abducted While in the
   Service of Stanley in Search of
      Emin Pasha at Juba and Was
 Taken Prisoner by Cannibals in Manyuema
 and Was Given My Freedom by Chief Ngombi
 and in Possession of a Rare Blue Diamond
   Explored the Savage Pygmy Forest and
      Discovered the Uncommon Element
              Ekwateurium


              David I. Silvermann
                 Vienna 1896
```

Frequently during my initiation, I awakened from the depths of unconscious, my head full of vivid yet ephemeral dreams implanted by Barthelme Nzombi Ngoi. Very old, withered like fruit partly eaten and tossed aside, the clever sorcerer's feeble appearance could not mask the unmistakable power of his aggressive eyes, eyes you could not escape if once they looked into your own. Given the name Barthelme years before by a

British missionary he would kill with a bolt of lightning, the villagers called him Nzombi because he had visited death, Ngoi because he returned to life as a Leopard Man. Ever afterward, if afraid or set upon by enemies, especially certain *féticheurs* who coveted the sorcerer's powerful gris-gris, Barthelme would transform into a ferocious, black and tawny cat.

Normal reality dissolved like sugar in the sea as I devoted every waking moment to reconstructing the minutia of Barthelme's dreams. My initiation began when the brown Sorcerer opened fresh wounds across my chest with a deadly viper, raking its fangs across the furrows of my already disfigured flesh. The hideous serpent's poison entered my wounds in measured surges each time Barthelme exerted pressure on oily, dark green tattoos covering the serpent's sleek head, which remained immobilized by the sorcerer's crippled fingers. For days afterward, my festering wounds burned with venom. Near death with snake fever, under the relentless spell of the dream seen through the eyes of the Leopard Man, I swooned in and out of consciousness, delirious, helpless.

"Truth," Barthelme trolled, his voice an indigo mist, "is a riddle and a talking serpent."

"Truth," I responded from deep inside the Earth, mimicking his roiling bellow, "is a riddle, after-death amassed across the moist floor of the great forest, Bushong."

"Truth," the Sorcerer continued, his words and their significance striking in disconnected rubato, "is a riddle, but not the drummer dancing you."

"Truth," I sang, "is a riddle, a riddle whose answer is the un-hollowed drum growing in the heart of a Wenge tree spurned by the termite queen, Saba Saba."

The old man carefully traced my mouth with his finger, painting me crimson where I chanted, blood red paint tasting of rock salt crushed in a rusty crucible.

"Truth," Barthelme screeched, "is a riddle never spoken, nor sung, nor carved from ash in the stick words of missionaries!"

"Truth," I added, tearing a page from the Book of Spells, crumpling it into a tiny ball and dropping it into the verdant flames of a dream, causing an explosion of blinding white fire, "is a riddle the length of a broken thread sewn through the lips of God."

"Truth," Barthelme chanted, sprinkling potent herbs over the fire, causing a storm of bright sparks and smoke sweet fog, "is a riddle, is flesh, is rock, is forest, is river, is the unifying sky whose answer cannot be found in songs about flesh, rock, forest, river or the dividing sky."

"Truth," I concluded, "is the riddle of liars whose answer is repeated by cowards afraid to dream of cloudy magic and Molimo."

My dream, my initiation, lasted for an imponderable number of weeks, which I passed without leaving Gongo-Yembe-Bobo-wa-Isiri. The tiny village, rimmed by reedy marshes bordering lazy rivers, sown into a small bosquet, seemed a loving parasite, a mate seeking bee trapped in an abundance of anther. The compact language of the people of Gongo-Yembe-Bobo-wa-Isiri echoed the surrounding forest called Bushong, the black-water sea, Mai-Ndombe, the murmuring swamp known as the Marsh of Sleep, or the dream called Djobe. An omnipotent natural force, whose name they pronounced Molimo, first sang in their tongue.

"Be careful, the swamp speaks Animal," the villagers liked to caution. "The swamp speaks a language often confused with the particular speech of leopard, antelope, crocodile, crow and monkey. But the swamp speaks the language of the land, a language understood by birds and fish, serpents, elephants, jackals and pygmies alike." Barthelme, who had entered the swamp and returned, repeatedly warned me that to listen to the Animal song of Molimo was to sleep forever, unaware even that you were no longer awake.

The wrinkled sorcerer would laugh and say to me, "If you think you understand what the swamp has said, that means you are trapped in a dream, never to reawaken, your body transforming slowly into humid soil, alive, not alive, heartless, Nzombi."

Pondering such thoughts, Gbabendu and I often wandered through the village to escape my Queen's frequent fits of weeping and melancholy accompanied by the inarticulate raving of her immobilized nurse. With no transecting streets inside Gongo-Yembe-Bobo-wa-Isiri, the tiny village presented me with a disorienting maze of self-similarity. The huts, women's kitchens, men's *corps de gardes*, fruit trees and canals were arranged such that you could not walk ten paces in any direction without having to pivot, walk in another direction and enter a village identical to the village you had just passed through. Destination, I observed, mimicked the path taken as well as the point of origin. Thus, though Gongo-Yembe-Bobo-wa-Isiri was very small, home to fewer than fifty families, a nest of nests within a nest, one could easily stroll inside the village for hours without being sure if one had retraced one's steps, without once knowing one's position for certain.

Seven gates, green bamboo arches arranged along the thorny hedge marking the perimeter of Gongo-Yembe-Bobo-wa-Isiri, allowed egress to various parts of the forest. Primarily women, children and hunters used the Four Gates of Hunger, Gates numbered Two, Four, Five and Seven. These led to plantations, animal traps, hunting grounds and fishponds. Only initiates used the Sorcerer's exit, called simply the Third Gate, passing through it on the way to a secluded river marsh where we practiced magic. Barthelme Nzombi Ngoi lived beside the river. His hut of tree bark and palm fronds perched on bamboo stilts above the weed clotted, slow moving water of a dark slough at the end of the path beginning at the Third Gate.

The Sixth Gate to Nowhere, as its name implied, led deep into the jungle of blackened shadows and knotted caves. Villagers used the sixth portal only when there was a death, or if someone had gone missing. Since evil intentions produced death and disappearance, however, even the oldest, wisest villagers exercised great prudence when using the Sixth Gate to Nowhere, lest someone accuse them of falsely accusing another of doing evil.

The First Gate, called Djobe, led north along the western shore of Black-water, Mai-Ndombe. The villagers instructed me that Djobe was a great and powerful beast, brother of the Sun and father of the Moon. The murmuring Marsh of Sleep recounted his exploits. The oldest and youngest villagers alike agreed that deadly blue serpents, serpents whose eyes shone with diamonds brighter than sunlight striking the back of a black water snake, slept in Djobe's enormous, dark belly. Serpent worshiping spearmen who entrap interlopers with shrewd riddles before transforming them into snakes, they cautioned in the tone used when speaking of the enchanting language of the swamp, guard the under-swamp.

During my lengthy initiation, I used four different Gates. I first entered the village through the Sixth Gate to Nowhere after wandering lost for many weeks with my Sphere and my Queen. After purchasing my initiation with Great Chief Ngombi's diamonds, village children led me daily through one of the Four Gates of Hunger to bathe in quiet pools of dark water. They cleansed my flesh with soap made from tree bark chewed and spit back into the red swamp, bailing the oily mix over me with their tiny hands. All the while, the children related stories about the Seven Gates of Gongo-Yembe-Bobo-wa-Isiri, the strange Leopard Man, Nzombi Ngoi, the Marsh of Sleep, the Riddle of the Swamp, darkest Djobe and the beast within.

I exited through the Third Gate to Nzombi Ngoi's dark lair only once, the day after my arrival, the day he implanted a ponderous dream using a poisonous serpent. Late that night, swooning under dream filled fever, I returned through the same Gate. Many weeks later, when the initiation had ended and I was well enough to make the journey to Djobe, the oldest villager, a shrunken man named Baoso Kiri, led me through the First Gate followed by Barthelme, Rafiki Kalele, and a handful of trusted warriors. We marched the entire day through swamps bordering and often mingling with a shallow river. Before nightfall, the sun gazing passionately across the mist shrouded swamp, we boarded pirogues bobbing lazily at the edge of a great body of black water. The lake lay serene, windless. We voyaged north beneath a late day moon suspended proudly overhead, orange and soothing. I charted my journey along the western shore using a small steel needle cut from the blade of Gjinok's Sword. After calculating the angle of the setting sun, I inscribed my steel armillary's nocturnal bands with the date and time. Slowly, I counted seven-thousand and two-hundred cycles, marking the Sphere with the location of Procyon rising in advance of the blue dog, Sirius, and the sleepless hunter, Orion. My intention, to heat the steel rings later and pierce them to create settings for tiny shards of Grandfather Chaim's pommel ruby and Great Chief Ngombi's blue diamonds, forever marking my celestial beacons with terrestrial fire as I had done in Gongo-Yembe-Bobo-Wa-Isiri.

Night engulfed our heavy boats. We became mere dark stains on black water. The eye of the moon led the hand of the painter who stroked the tips of ebony waves, secreting white light to guide us to the northern point of Mai-Ndombe. Throughout the languorous voyage, Barthelme lay on his back in a shallow puddle of bilge swamping our pirogue, snoring contentedly, both eyes open wide, twin moons of bread dough. For my part, I continued busily inscribing the Sphere with arcane characters representing the intersection of my voyage's stars with the sleeping Sorcerer's esoteric grunts.

Soon after first light, we paddled into a narrow channel clotted with broad leaves further choking the lazy current of the Olongo Nule. Even before we reached the river Mantaba and penetrated the edge of Palus Somni, I could hear the garrulous soporific of yawning speech bubbling up from the weedy muck beneath our boats. We hacked and paddled several hours through dense overgrowth choking the river before rounding a wide bend to discover Gongo-Pende, a sultry village of grass enclosures lashed to heavy dock poles wobbling gently over the water. A fierce Pygmy spearman directed us to remain inside one of the huts until the Chief, accompanied by an entourage of painted warriors, came for us.

Sensing my trepidation at seeing so many fearsome weapons brandished by dark skinned spearmen, the Chief explained the barbed spears. "We use them to trap serpents so that venom, fangs, blood and eggs can be safely harvested without harming the revered reptiles."

Barthelme Nzombi Ngoi announced, "The tattooed white man, Ndakabwa of Shiloh, is your friend. He is very wise and possesses incantations of rare magic. He comes in peace and hopes to visit the dream of Djobe, for which I have carefully and rigorously prepared him." The Sorcerer nudged me. I fumbled with one of my blue diamonds.

The Chief spearman smiled revealing dark teeth filed to sharp points. Adorned with herpetic fetishes, he wore fingerless gloves of boa skin and matching boots, a necklace of snake bones around his neck. Rings and bracelets made from snake fangs circled his arms and lower legs. The spearmen argued among themselves, hissing and often spitting or slapping their thighs to add emphasis. When the debate reached a strident pitch, the Chief looked candidly into my eyes. "No mzungus," he hissed. No whites.

I first reacted with disbelief then tried to explain that sooner or later the Chief and his people would be forced to submit to the insatiable curiosity of whites who would explore and exploit the continent in greater numbers with each passing year. Rafiki advised me to use a different argument. Baoso Kiri explained that the spearmen of the swamp had seen the smoking boats of white men on the great river to the north, black bearers squeezed onto the decks among crates of cargo and animals. They had vowed then and there never to permit whites into the Marsh of Sleep, nor to allow the white man to haul their people upriver on burning barges like boxes and goats.

I explained that I had no intention of forcing anyone to ride upriver, that I had been upriver with Henry Stanley's expedition in search of Emin Pasha, and that as a result I had become convinced that such expeditions were a folly inspired by greed and the arrogant desire for individual celebrity. The

Chief debated with his spearmen again. One young warrior in particular appeared loath to compromise the tribal ban against white men entering the swamp. Writhing with wild, threatening gestures, biting the air like a serpent striking at a rat, he evidently persuaded the Chief who repeated the words, "No mzungus!"

Having traveled far to find the spearmen's primitive enclave, I fully intended to find Djobe. Still, to encounter a people so completely oblivious of the surrounding world seething with its white soldiers, surveyors, merchants and governors in search of profitable trading colonies, greatly surprised me. Only arrogance prevented me from leaving and returning with vulgar, Belgian soldiers of the sort who had twice murdered Gongo Lutete. However, I had come with peaceful intentions. I desperately bared my chest to display scars of the horror I had endured at the hands of my Luba brothers. I produced the fabulous Sphere of my fabrication. Pygmy warriors leapt back as I rotated the bands sparkling with tiny stars of broken rubies and blue diamond shards tracing my long journey.

"I have seen your world. Read my scars and tattoos. They are stars. I am one of you now. I have eaten your food, slept with your women, gone to war with your men, commuted with your Gods. I have shed my own blood freely and I have hungrily devoured the flesh of your enemies!"

Barthelme Nzombi Ngoi admonished the spearmen. "The village of Gongo Pende will prosper with many strong, male children borne by fertile women fed by plentiful wild fish and game," he boasted, "if you will permit Ndakabwa to enter the Marsh of Sleep."

The Chief argued with the stubborn young spearman again, ending the discussion by striking the defiant one in the head with the side of a bone knife. "There is a way to decide if you should be allowed onto our land," advised the Chief. "You must speak with the serpents and answer a Riddle posed by the swamp."

My heart stopped. I protested in forbidding whispers to Barthelme. The Sorcerer reassured me that my initiation had prepared me for just such a test. He assured me that I could not explore Djobe without first talking to serpents. I had no choice. That night, while the others drank a brown, foul smelling potion after a meal of monkey and pangolin, I sat alone in darkness. The strange liquid caused my companions and spearmen alike to drowse in their own vomit. Minutes later they became animated, agitated and eventually extremely boisterous. In this state of menace, the Pygmy spearmen hoisted me over their heads and carried me into the moonlit fen.

Unable to see but the broken monstrance of moon netted by deformed trees, I had no sense of my path, neither direction nor destination. The intoxicated spearmen chattered, spat, hissed, laughed lewdly, and then, without warning, hurled me roughly through the night. I spilled over and over in the pitch like a sack of apples in a damp cellar. Long, wriggling bodies began to squirm beneath me. A large sausage slowly pulled itself free from under my buttocks. Small, wormy black serpents swarmed across my legs and hands, carrying the light of the moon, attempting in vain to slither up my sweat oiled limbs. Praying the test would quickly end if I refrained from screaming or lunging toward an escape, I sat up among the snakes as still as stone.

Spearmen lit torches atop poles spaced evenly around a deep, circular pit, precisely in the middle of which I sat, paralyzed by the most abject horror I had ever experienced. Suffering the paralysis of silence, my mind fixed dangerously on the murmuring swamp. I fought the desire to listen to its soothing voice. Hundreds upon hundreds of slithering, entangled, hissing bodies of all sizes and markings crawled upon me. Dominant serpents surrounded me, testing my body with their fluttering tongues. A black forest cobra rose to a great height, threatening the muddy spearmen yellowed by torch light above, forcing them to retreat from the edge of the pit. Spewing like vomit from the slime, a giant green mamba struck at a spearman's bare stomach. A swamp python skidded heavily across my legs, working its way up my arm until its head lay on my shoulder, its mouth close to my ear.

"Be calm. I will not bite you," the python said, "But I will crush you if you move."

"What do you want?" I asked.

"Just one thing. Tell me, if you are permitted to explore this land, do you intend to destroy us?"

"The serpents?" I hastened.

"The land! I prefer to eat small animals, babies are best. I hunt in the trees. The trees live in the swamp, like the spearmen. We are one animal, the swamp and the serpents and the spearmen."

"I want to explore Djobe. That is all."

"But Djobe is not yours to explore," said the python, extending a portion of its body through the air to have a look at my face, most of its bulk poised uncomfortably upon my shoulder. After studying me carefully, the great serpent lowered itself, as if attached to the cable of an invisible davit, then spilt languidly into a turgid knot of dark serpents gathered around me.

I felt a rubbery nose poke rudely the back of my neck, obliging me to turn my head. I shifted my eyes to a green mamba's binocular tongue dancing upon my nose. The magnificent serpent hissed, "Tssss."

"What do you want?" I asked, deathly frightened of a serpent whose bite would certainly doom me before anyone could intervene.

"You," replied the snake in a female voice, "I want to touch you. Don't be afraid."

The towering mamba teetered but remained erect, its head quivering atop a plume of sinew. Its symmetrically scarred head level with my eyes, supported by the coiled river of its lower body, the glistening snake collapsed against the side of my head, hooked its delicate body over my shoulder, writhed to mount me, dragging its endless tail behind. Effortlessly raising opal eyes, the mamba touched my face with its nose, baring its fangs, exposing the satiny inner surface of its mouth as it explored my intricate facial scars, my sweat, moving slowly down my body to my genitals, my toes.

"Do you think I am pretty?" asked the snake.

"You are quite beautiful, the epitome of feminine and masculine, of animal and vegetable, of sensual desire for life and mortal dread of death's deprivation," I answered.

"Deprivation? Life is death, Ndakabwa, but desire is not deprivation. Do you not agree?" The mamba punctured my neck without driving its fangs deep into my muscle, then released a trace of venom. My throat constricted instantaneously, causing my heart to race wildly. "Do you still think I am pretty?"

"Yes," I choked forth, "for the reasons I gave you."

The mamba drooped over my shoulder and crawled across my back as venom slowly stiffened my body. I tried to relax, to breathe evenly, hoping to minimize the effect of poison thickening my blood. The mamba gazed into my eyes once again. "Do you love me?"

Unsure of what to say, I groped for an allegory or a metaphor, something indirect to appease the deadly serpent, but I could only think of the truth, "No," I stammered.

"No?" The green mamba threatened to strike, focused, taut, a steel cable straining toward a single purpose.

"No, I detest you, serpent! I fear your touch, now get off me!" I clawed the words. Shrugging with all my might, I cast off the mamba, listening fearfully as its green body smacked the wet pit floor with a slap while acrid venom cemented my joints.

The mamba looked up. "You don't know who you are or what you want," it said, slipping through a briar of small vipers and racers wrestling under my legs, disappearing among thousands of snaking serpents, essing and hissing, slippery, slithering, cold blooded.

I moved my eyes around carefully, praying for the test to end. I wanted to weep and quit, I wanted to leap up and escape from the hell of the awful snake pit. My greatest fear was the one onerous obligation I could not shake, that I would foolishly endure any torment in order to achieve my purpose. What had begun as a self-respecting matter of base pride and misunderstood courage, the son, the man, the explorer, the assassin, the conqueror, had become a desperate attempt to pass Africa's fundamental, final test of simple survival.

A third serpent spoke. "The Riddle of the Swamp is one word, Truth. Speak me the answer, Daka Bwana of Shiloh!"

I turned slowly and gazed into the fiery eyes of a strange viper whose scarlet mouth contained hideous, dark mammalian teeth sharpened to triangular points. Quickly realizing that the Chief spearman had miraculously transmuted into the viper before me, I almost swooned. A torrent of anger poured through me, "I don't know how to answer your Riddle!"

"Ndakabwa, what is a riddle but the obvious answer to a deceptive question you have never considered? How can you escape a trap whose jaws you do not feel? TRUTH, Ndakabwa? The land belongs to itself. In its heart is the Animal to whom we belong. The Animal must remain free to choose those who may survive upon its breast and those who will not. If the land cannot balance all things, the land will die."

"I am an explorer." I spoke calmly, trying to steady my mind. "I come in peace, in the name of a great race searching for more land, more resources to feed the bellies and minds of its superior civilization. Allow us to explore freely and we shall free you from your ignorance."

"The land is the only freedom I desire. It is complete. The enlightenment you offer will only take away my land and return forgetfulness. You see, you are the jaws of the trap that traps you. You are the answer to the Riddle of the Swamp."

"We can share the land! There is more than enough!"

"You are not listening!" the serpent screeched. "Freedom is not infinite but limited to a few. Freedom does not extend indefinitely, as you naively imply. Cut one tree, kill one serpent, hinder me from taking revenge against my enemy, then you have taken away the freedom bestowed upon me by my ancestors."

"As you say, freedom is finite, depending as much on the boundaries it imposes as the autonomy it maintains. But my ancestors have never been free. Civilization itself is infernal bondage," I argued, ashamed that I could not offer greater dialectic. "Once unearthed, your people must be refined, like ore. As for me, I must continue to explore freely. So goes civilization."

"You are right, Ndakabwa, my land will not render greater freedom to you. You can only diminish my freedom and strengthen the shackles holding you responsible for the actions of your civilization, for the corrupt culture of your grandchildren."

"If you cannot understand the price of knowledge, perhaps you do not deserve to be free!" I bellowed.

"Why? What is the connection between knowledge and freedom? Until you came, Ndakabwa, the price of freedom was learning the languages of other animals, other tribes. My ancestors came here from deep inside the forest. There was no one, only serpents. We built our huts in the trees above the swamp and listened carefully to its heartbeat. This land belongs to us because we came here first!"

"No, you are mournfully ignorant and sadly wrong. My ancestors discovered the magic of counting and the science of multiplication! My ancestors captured the power of lightning, the music of the heartbeat, the heat of the sun, the center of the earth, the bottom of the ocean and the emptiness between the stars! My ancestors came here at the beginning of time, and everything we are capable of imagining, heavens and circles, belongs to us!"

The serpent wound around me several times, clearing away the other snakes before rising to whisper in my ear. "Then my people will multiply using our own magic for counting. And one day, my children, in prodigious numbers, Ndakabwa, with their prodigious appetites, will overrun your children and their superior minds. Your grandchildren will pay for the crimes of their ancestors. My grandchildren, with their superior purpose, will devour them. This I promise you if you attempt to take our land away or to take us away from our land."

"Chief, listen to me. I am a serpent among serpents and spearmen, am I not? Like you, I search for little more than the simplest answer to the Riddle of Truth." I rotated the Sphere slowly before my eyes, shifting the position of the many bands pierced with stars, inscribed with the tiny characters of my secret *alphabeta*. Indifferent to hundreds of slithering monsters entwining my lower body in ropes of sinew and slime, I began to shrink into the swamp of snakes, ever searching the Sphere for an answer. My throat tightened, my neck elongated until it was no thicker than a bamboo shoot, and the word was born, a sound which can be transliterated through proper orientation of the Sphere's character rings, but only approximated in print, "Ektsstke!"

"You are clever, Ndakabwa. Your word answers the Riddle," said the Chief.

"Truth is not a word to be uttered, viper, but a story told! Whether I live to explore Djobe or I decompose in mire, the Riddle of the Swamp has been answered. Truth? Ektsstke!"

"The word is TRUTH according to you. But truth is different for every man. If you truly understand this word, then act. You are free to explore the heart of the Animal. Go and explore the TRUTH you speak."

The black serpent's red mouth shrank away. My eyes fixed on an invisible star. A powerful spasm seized me, seized my every muscle, crushed my bones as it tied off sinew and tendon one by one to a steel post of most intense concentration. My flesh, my life, the path of my existence snapped, disentangled, whirled violently then condensed into an atom of matter. "Ektsstke!" I exploded.

I remember slipping effortlessly through knot after knot of crawling flesh and deadly beast. The spearmen hissed and spat their nasty spittle in the muck. I slithered up over the rim of the pit. An angry warrior pinned me to the ground with the long, curved barb of his spear.

"Let the serpent go," shouted the Chief.

"Let the serpent go into the Marsh of Sleep," cried Barthelme Nzombi Ngoi. "Ndakabwa has spoken with the serpents. He is free to explore!"

The frightened spearman raised his barb, allowing me to skulk on my belly into the darkness. Once beyond the reach of spearmen, I raced madly against the Riddle of the Swamp and the Spell of Truth. My vestigial legs began to grow back, my arms. Soon, I ran erect again along an unlit path, shedding my serpent skin, ignoring the voices of Barthelme and the others withering behind me. I concentrated fully on the murmuring swamp guiding my snaking fingers as they feverishly transcribed every syllable into symbols on the rings of my brilliant Sphere. Speeding euphorically naked through the Marsh of Sleep, suddenly I spied the entrance to Djobe, an ignominious puncture in a mound of Earth, a root bound pustule of bluish mud oozing above the level of the swamp. Minutes later, I was joined by my breathless companions led by my trusted companion, Rafiki.

A natural embankment appeared to have been forced upward from below behind a small, dense object. After removing much of the detritus, I succeeded in squeezing down the narrow passageway. Djobe's throat resembled a sheaf of paper rolled tightly and unevenly, narrow for most of its length, noticeably wider at the bottom than at the top. I crawled toward a source of light far below. The surrounding walls wept mud for some distance before their composition changed to coal, pure, silky black coal.

I estimated the downward slope to be approximately thirty degrees measured from the vertical. Eventually, the passage widened enough for me to stand up, and later, enough to extend my arms overhead. Though my body had reassembled slowly into the shape of a man, time had grown strangely distorted, trapping my perceptions between the dreams of serpent and man. Minutes may have been seconds or hours. Unable to determine the depth of my descent due to the powerful illusion of timelessness beneath the swamp, I entered a vault resembling the flared bowl of an inverted funnel tipped slightly sideways. Still some distance below, a ledge of coal extended round the perimeter of an enormous crater shimmering mysteriously, radiant and blue. I signaled the others to move carefully. We descended together until, perched on the rim of infinite darkness, I summoned the courage to look into the depths. Rafiki held my ankles. Nzombi held Rafiki's ankles. Old Baoso Kiri held Nzombi's ankles. Thus, I lowered myself over the edge to have a peek. From that precarious vantage, I first gazed into the belly of Djobe.

For hundreds of meters below, as far as I could see, coils of darkly glowing mineral wound like an elegant spiral staircase lit with black burning tapers. In honor of my ungrateful Queen, I gave the name Ekwateurium to the uncommon element acting as cement binding an aggregate of blue diamonds. Ekwateurium appeared dull yet glowed the blackest black imaginable. Frequent pockets of shattered diamond crystal near the wall's surface created the illusion that Ekwateurium glowed with eerie light. Steady precipitation originating from the swamp above rained into the cavern creating a brilliant black rainbow arcing wraithlike, there and not there, deep into the bowels of the Earth.

I signaled Rafiki to pull me up and promptly ordered my companions to the surface. Barthelme Nzombi Ngoi, objected. "Daka Bwana, we must take one of the diamonds and a handful of the glowing blackness to prove we discovered Djobe. Otherwise, no one will believe you."

I argued that plucking even one diamond from the many eyes of Djobe would be too dangerous. "We will return with ropes made from liana, tools fashioned from spears, and a solid container for transporting Ekwateurium and diamonds." My plan made sense until Barthelme reminded me that the Chief and his spearmen would throw all of us to the snakes if we returned without proof of our heroic descent.

Rafiki volunteered. "Put me over the rim. I am the smallest. Baoso Kiri can hold my feet, Nzombi his feet, and Ndakabwa, you are the biggest, you will anchor me like a tree."

We squirmed into position. Rafiki and Baoso Kiri both disappeared out of sight, head down in a gaseous cavern aglow with blue diamonds and rare Dark Earth. The task of pulling my companions out proved extremely arduous as I strained to inch backwards on my knees and elbows. Nzombi did the same. First out came Baoso Kiri, whose expression seemed luminous but relieved. Then came Rafiki, who struggled to clutch only one or two grains weighing more than a curbstone. A handful of diamonds rolled beneath as we pulled him out of the glowing black hole on his belly.

The climb to the surface was torturous, one thousand meters, perhaps more. Rafiki stubbornly insisted on carrying the burden of tiny grains in his hands all the way to the top. Day and swamp greeted me first, blowing a cool breeze and cleansing rain. We found thirty spearmen led by the stubborn young warrior waiting for us. Baoso Kiri looked haggard as he stepped into the light of day. A spearman rudely snatched the few diamonds he carried. Last out was Rafiki whose very appearance caused the spearmen to recoil down the mound into swamp mire that licked their ankles thickly. The skin on Rafiki's arms, chest and brow, anywhere the dark glow of Ekwateurium had touched him, fell from his bones like overcooked gazelle. Though critically burned, he still clutched several particles of the uncommon element.

The spearmen argued frantically with their young leader whether to kill Rafiki, or to kill all of us, or none of us, or just me. Then, without alarm, the leader hurled his spear, burying its barbed tip deep in Rafiki's chest so that the point could be seen sticking out of his sweating back as he fell.

Dropping the poisonous Ekwateurium, my friend of so many adventures gasped, "Ndakabwa, you must recognize the true Queen of Sena Tatu, attain your destiny with her, then return, destroy these serpents. The land is ours!" Rafiki's fluids wept freely as his eyes closed for the last time.

I cursed the spearman, lurching in the leader's direction only to be blinded by an army of barbed spears. "You have the diamonds!" I screamed. "What more do you want? Do you want more? Follow me, then. Let's go!"

The young warrior grabbed another spear, hurling the weapon with such force that the barbed tip drove loudly through Basso Kiri's chest, causing the old man's heart and lungs to burst out of his back. Barthelme Nzombi Ngoi's eyes turned amber. He howled fiendishly, briefly sending the spearmen back into the swamp water as he twisted horribly, his flesh flying off like festering scales, his bones snapping. Before the Sorcerer could transmogrify completely into a leopard, ten spears slaughtered the feral beast.

The swamp men screeched vile curses and blood chilling war whoops. Tempted by fear to drop to my knees and beg for mercy, I caught a glimpse of the Chief spearman emerging from the rear of the mob walking upright, smiling, exposing his sharpened teeth. I listened to the voice of anger once again and hissed the mystical word, "Ektsstke!" before lunging over Rafiki's corpse, scooping up the ponderously heavy grains and diving headlong into Djobe's maw. I plunged in an unbroken fall hundreds of meters downward, the astringent smell of Ekwateurian effluvium the only sensation I could recognize as I tumbled over the final ledge and into the soul of the Animal to whom we belong.

Experiencing pain more excruciating than any scarring, tattoo or poison arrow while infinitesimal pin pricks of matter punctured my flesh, I passed clean through my body. Suddenly weightless, I felt not one sensation of plummeting down, but rather imagined floating upward. My mind argued that I would eventually strike bottom and burst like a sack of bones. Before me, I saw only blackness, inviting emptiness, sensual forgetfulness and nothing, absolute-nothing. Then, appallingly unprepared, I collided with Self and Truth.

Pulverized into a tiny ball, my eyes witnessed the contrary. My torso and limbs stretched impossibly until I appeared to myself rope-like, a mad tangle of gangling entrails. In the time it took to blink my leaden eyes, I vanished from my mind and reappeared outside the mortal body, incredibly free of sensuality. In a viscous miasma of black aether, I had become a grain of blue starlight. Fear ceased to exist. My consciousness functioned as a mooring, allowing me to remember that the recipient of the fantastic sensations was I. Oblivious of knowledge, memory, character, I focused intensely into my immortal soul. What I did not understand, however, during this period of suspended perception, was that I continued to fall, to undergo subtle changes as I neared the far side of the blackest black ocean.

Once again passage was violently sensory, memorable in the extreme. Most vividly, I remember striking the bottom. Bottom, the abstract idea of bottom in a hole as yet unexcavated, embedded itself in my mind like ragged shrapnel. I lay there on my back, looking up from the blackness into swirling nothing overhead, black blacker than darkness, opening and shutting my eyes. Through the invisible soup of emptiness, I saw a light, not a globe or a disk but a lunar sliver entering the new moon phase. I realized, like Kepler, that I had voyaged far from the Earth, far from home, far inside the Animal, to the very center where beats its black-most heart. I invoked the Biblic Sorcery of the Book of Spells, screaming, "God made two great lights; the greater light to rule the day, and the lesser light to rule the night: he made the stars also!"

The aether remained empty and cold. Prepared to resign myself to entering eternity alone, in darkness, I blinked again, halting the rotating eclipse, capturing the moon as it moved into the first quarter. Immobilized by despair, I cradled the Glorious Sphere in my hands, its steel bands subtly less dark than the aether. I adjusted the meridians in frenzy, hoping to capture light in the moveable shards of diamond and ruby, entreating Djobe to reveal me a sign, to blow a warm breath over my frozen body. Sweat poured from my brow as I calibrated the metal bands, blinded by blackness, unable to read my own, wildly esoteric notations. I blinked. Kepler's somnolent lunar orb would soon be full. Working hysterically, I pulled the rings together, creating a nearly solid hemisphere of steel smelted and forged by Grandfather into Gjinok's

Sword. It had beheaded Abdulla Suliman, murdered Lisboa and Emin Pasha and loyally slaughtered Arab slavers at the side of Gongo Lutete. Alone on the bank of the Sankuru River, I had heated the fearsome blade with the fire of Spells, cut steel with the sword's broken tip and hammered until the Sphere of Mind and Knowledge was created. Holding the powerful orb against my throat, I waited for a pulse of remembrance from the heart of the Animal. I blinked, halting the great dark hole of emptiness and sleep. Kepler's Moon emerged from blackness full. "I claim the Lesser Light by the authority of the Animal to whom we belong!" I screamed.

The finger of Yawah writing his commandments in Sinai granite for Moise, Djobe hurled beams of black light against the hemispheric shield of the Sphere, inscribing all of the information contained, the complete memory of the hole of emptiness. The Sphere glowed brightly, its blue diamonds and ruby stars illuminating the belly of It-Self at the instant of resplendence. Guided by blindness, my eyes moved to an opening in the solid wall of black-black Ekwateurium, a dark portal. I crawled toward it over painful alluvium deposited by the spinning aether of emptiness. Before ducking into the rocky cranny, I blinked again, blinding the darkness for one last time. The great astronomer's yawning ebony moon, eclipsed by the blacker-than-black, third quarter sun of man, vanished!

My Sphere shone dully, written riotously with the histories of individual particles of the stars, like me, bounded by the belly of the heavens free within. Before escaping the cavern for the icy solitude of sweating pipes, I reached down and seized a single grain of interminable blackness. A tremendous surge of mental acuity overcame me. I dropped the tiny stone inside the Sphere and closed the metal bands over steel ribs confining the heart of the Animal we were.

I started to run along a semi dark corridor but suddenly stopped to shout again the word, "Ektsstke!" The Sphere vibrated in my hands like a newborn pup. The energy I received served me well for I walked up and down endless days in an inky ice storm without food or water. Up steep stony ramps I trudged hoping to break the surface only to round the crest and trundle down another mud slick slope. Up. Down, down, down. Up. I feared the extraordinary climbs would not offset the cumulative, depressing descents. Then, without premonition, without signal or indication of any kind, I turned a corner, stepped upon a rock and found myself at the surface of the Earth. My head lay directly mid-threshold beneath the Sixth Gate to Nowhere. My eyes looked into those of my children, the ever pouting, seven fingered Queen and the radiant Gbabendu. Saba wept and cursed me for leaving her. Gbabendu smiled and handed me a trembling white bird. Suddenly, just as Rafiki had predicted, I recognized that Gbabendu, the child of Sena Mbili, was my true Queen.

Fighting back revulsion, that night I chewed a tiny morsel of Doctor Bwana David's shriveled heart. When I'd eaten half, I could already feel taking root the metamorphosis from Professor to Prophet. I whispered solemnly for the moon to lurch backwards, for time to run in reverse, for tomorrow to become yesterday. Then, without removing the stone from the madwoman's ankle, I whispered goodbye to Nbulu and slit her throat. In the corner of my eye, I saw Gbabendu stab the seven fingered child again and again, forever putting an end to Emin Pasha's perfidy. My true Queen skillfully removed the girl's heart and reverently devoured it.

I partook of another bite of Bwana Livingstone's death and sketched in the dirt with a stick a precise map of the heavens superimposed upon a crude projection of the Earth's surface, mimicking the orbiting bands of my splendid memory Sphere. Sena Tatu, I called it, in honor of the third capitol of the wandering spirit. Later, I washed Emin's wicked liqueur from Gbabendu's fingers with my tongue. Following Kepler's instructions, I adjusted the bands of the marvelous Sphere and pushed the delicate thumb of my tattooed Queen between Procyon and Sirius. Clamping the bands tightly together in my hand, Gbabendu's black digit popped off like a well-cooked chicken wing. I continued inserting her soft digits into the Gjinok's jaws and carefully removed three fingers from her small hands, three toes from her delicate feet until she transformed fully from orphan to Saba, Mother of Us All.

"My Queen," I whispered over and over, gently wiping her tears, binding her wounds in moss and leaves. "Queen Saba."

I consumed another sliver of Saint Livingstone's organ then lay beside my sleeping Queen. I could not rest. The jungle's breath blew cool though I perspired feverishly, siphoning deep, measured gasps to keep from suffocating. David Livingstone's soul thrashed in my otherwise empty belly, alive again, Nzombi. I retched pungent bile and swallowed it, retched again and again swallowed, chewing over and over the grizzle of his Bitter Heart until only blackened saliva stained my bloody, burning tongue.

3. The Flying Horse

A n invisible shroud enveloped Dar es Salaam, humid silk the color of sky and sea, almost white but blue, pale blue. "Like the heat of Daytona Beach, Florida," muttered Tonio, the gold miner from Arusha, "but for the stinking-linger of spoiled market fish and bloody seaweed rotting on dhows keeled over just there." His sweat lacquered leather chin, darkened with whisker-stubble, jerked towards a dirty blanket of beach discarded at the mouth of the slate-colored harbor.

Tonio studied container ships stacked high, red, blue, orange quilts sharing the horizon with steel grey vessels languishing heavy with grain in shark-infested seas out beyond the reef waiting for an open berth at the port. From where he stood beneath dry, rusty cedars guarding the footpath alongside Ocean Road, he could see clean across the bay. Late nineteenth century seafarers were wisely seduced into moving operations from their notorious, oceanside slave terminal at Bagamoyo, down the white sand - brown coral coast to the naturally formed Harbor of Peace, Dar es Salaam.

Knowing both waterfronts—Bagamoyo's sand bottom bay gently-sloping as if scooped out by hand, and Dar's sheltered clamshell cove—Tonio approved the decision by the Sultan of Zanzibar to develop Dar es Salaam just over a century earlier, smiling at history's generous irony. The Sultan's new East African center was quickly expropriated by *Gesellschaft Deutsche für Kolonisation,* the German trading company, who lost it to the British after the First World War, who then had to relinquish control to African socialists at independence. Tonio pursed thin Sicilian lips inherited from his father, nodded to the phantom alter ego he always, as long as he could remember, conferred with, and disdainfully counted seventeen out-of-service cranes in the distance, leaving just three to handle Darport's twelve busy berths. Dock workers cannibalized conveyors, augers and baggers to offload hundreds of thousands of tons of grain for drought victims in the scorched savannas of Southern Africa. Hundreds of thousands of dollars' worth of four-wheel-drive vehicles for the ever-increasing number of expatriates: aid workers, diplomats and businessmen like himself dangled from mobile cranes on dirty slings.

"If only Tony were Director General, the port would function like a jet fighter," he chuckled to himself, winking arrogantly for the benefit of his phantom friend. "Few port managers have studied aerospace engineering at Embry-Riddle. And even if they have, how many are the good looking Afro-Italian-type?" Tonio poked the air as though his alter ego might leap the way his Ugandan house boy Idi jumped when properly threatened. "Where is the Flying Horse?" he hissed, trudging across the sand munching boiled peanuts from a wad of twisted brown sack paper dusted with cement. Careful not to exert himself any more than necessary, Tonio climbed the hill where the ragged edge of the street above had years before washed away leaving a rusted sewer pipe dripping with foul, orange sludge for local laborers to wash in.

Sauntering along the street behind the Central Bank of Tanzania and the towering Kilimanjaro Hotel, Tonio flaunted his jewelry among the throng of far less affluent African pedestrians. Gold chains studded with rubies and diamonds slung tantalizingly loose around Tonio's wrists and neck, he considered himself fearless having once beat senseless with a blunt *Panga* a thieving worker at his first gold mine for the crime of trying to steal a shovel. Spotting a young boy with polio gnarled legs trundling through the sand-clogged gutter on the calloused heels of his filthy black hands, Tonio stopped at a battery of wooden tables where hungry-eyed adults sold everything from soap to salted fish, bought sticky hard candy the size of a ping pong ball, and with a paternal smile, handed it, like a priest dispensing the Eucharist, to the crippled boy.

The Flying Horse was late leaving for the Spice Island of Zanzibar and Tonio could do nothing but wander alongside the road ringing the harbor, choked with pedestrians, and watch ships come and go, estimating salvage value of each rusting, half sunken hull littering the oil soaked ribbon of beach below, and wait, however impatiently, for the catamaran that would take him off shore for a business weekend arranged by a wealthy government minister anxious to open Zanzibar's port to Tonio's increasingly profitable smuggling activities.

Sweat saturated Tonio's cologne-soaked black silk shirt despite an aggressive sea breeze pawing at the button mast left open to his gaunt waist. "At ten-thirty," Tonio growled, "if the Flying Horse has not arrived, I am forgetting about Minister Salim and going home!"

Still pristine among the ragtag, mold blackened concrete office towers of Dar es Salaam, the unabashedly gaudy building housing the World Bank, several consulting firms and a block of luxury apartments, including Tonio's suite on the gold shield shaded windows of the twenty-first floor, rose above the dusty, red roofed skyline of government offices scattered on the bluff overlooking the harbor. Everything a businessman needed lay within a stone's throw—though plans to relocate the Tanzanian capital lock stock and barrel to the remote city of Dodoma remained on the books—the Parliament, Finance Ministry, Public Works, Health, Education, Tourism, the Department of Plan, Defense Headquarters, Customs, Energy and Mines. Just as Tonio's mind looked deep into the eyes of the phantom and dredged up unpleasant memories of establishing his business in these same whitewashed buildings, a lethargic crowd hugging stingy shade around the catamaran port suddenly came to life.

Tonio jogged over to a barrier of coral masonry broken by steady erosion of the harbor, peered down at the turquoise water and spotted an elegant 500 seat, twin hulled Zanzibar shuttle, the Flying Horse, idling dockside. Tonio bought a

Coke from a soda seller wearing rags, guzzled it slowly then strolled down saltwater slick concrete steps scattered like hippo's teeth on the hillside and mounted the aluminum gangplank to the Flying Horse, a first-class ticket pinched in his fingers.

While second class passengers scurried for seats and space to stow their bundles on the large lower deck, Tonio danced up sparkling white treads to the cozy, air-conditioned lounge just below the pilot house. Plopping onto a bright orange couch, the self-assured entrepreneur purchased two cans of lukewarm Tiger beer from a passing concessionaire. Then he sat there with a can in each hand, arms extended like a man holding dumbbells, savoring the transition from the rundown Dar port to the upscale first-class lounge on the Flying Horse. Goose bumps spread up his arm like a rash and a chill plunged down his spine as first-class passengers trickled into the spacious lounge, many of them Asian, members of Dar es Salaam's large and influential Indian community. Many were Swahili, tobacco-colored African Muslims, fewer were black Africans, mainly government officials, and finally a salting of Euro stock, expats most of them, as well as a couple of tourists off on holiday.

One woman in particular, tall, with dark hair and skin the color of nacre, caught his eye, then his ear. Judging from her clipped French, she was Belgian, Walloon. When Tonio tried to smile the phantom whispered that his nose was too big for such a toothy smile. Tonio's mouth twitched into an involuntarily arrogant sneer. The Belgian woman looked into the Afro-Italian's dark, beady eyes for a second then went about her business, scooting her bags behind a yellow couch, one of three circling a low table claimed by her traveling companions. Tonio stared long at smooth, slender legs pouring from khaki shorts like milk from a marble font. He studied the woman's nutmeg brown lips and peach colored chin. Unable to ignore their buoyancy, Tonio ogled the woman's breasts as they flirted subtly with her sleeveless, royal blue blouse. She had delicate hands and her fingers, stalks of baby asparagus dipped into blood, toyed with a glittering gold choker hanging slack around her supple neck. Tonio closed his eyes, sighed deeply and pushed the two barely cool beer cans against his temples.

By the time the Flying Horse departed for a ninety-minute cruise east-northeast to the Zanzibar archipelago, Tonio had inventoried the entire female population in first class, singling out a handful of women whose beauty rivaled that of the unforgettable Belgian. There were two Indian girls with jet black hair, skin oiled like expensive teak wearing dresses colored brightly with birds and flowers. A stunning Nordic woman wore a white sun suit that turned her long limbs into seasoned pine and set fire to her golden hair. A bare shouldered African woman with flawless skin as blue as the bottom of the sea out beyond the reef sat by herself swaddled in a red and yellow Dutch wax print. Then there was the American, Birkenstock sandals, a loose-fitting dirty olive-green tee shirt, baggy plaid shorts, an unwieldy Jansport backpack, her swarthy tan legs glowing red, no doubt from hiking across Dar in the brutal morning sun to reach the port, her thighs lately unshaved, thick muscled like a male sprinter. Tonio drank his beers, surveyed all the females again so as not to miss any beauty, bought more beers, sprawled out on the couch, cooled down, lectured the phantom in his mind.

"Sex and money, Tony, and cold beer, nothing much else matters more unless you count sleep." The American educated helicopter pilot, a veteran of the Italian peace keeping contingent assigned to the 1993 UN Operation Restore Hope in Somalia, fidgeted like a rat in laboratory terrarium. "Expensive cognac, fast cars, a firm mattress, in that order." Food mattered least to Tonio, always a skinny kid who, no matter how much he ate, could not grow muscle. The metabolic rigors of adulthood had put hair on his chest and thickened his sinewy arms but left him cursed with an ability to eat as much as he liked without gaining weight, but without satiation, or satisfaction even, ever. Never did he enjoy eating a big meal.

The Flying Horse suddenly bucked, launching two-thirds of the first-class passengers across the lounge in Tonio's direction. Most caught their balance and recoiled back into their seats with a gasp or a chuckle. The American woman however, harnessed to her heavy purple rip stop nylon backpack, careened off the Belgian woman who clutched the couch back to keep from appearing ungraceful, picked up speed and crashed headfirst into the Afro-Italian in an unbuttoned black silk shirt.

"Shit!" she exclaimed. "Sorry."

"No, no. The pleasure is mine." Tonio pawed the stocky woman's breasts gratuitously, gently pushing her backwards with an innocent smile. "Won't you have a seat? You've come all this way."

The dishwater blond American coed adjusted herself inside the straps and buckles of her load, cinching tight the unwashed cotton tee until every seam of her X-treme sports bra showed as vividly as the vein dissecting her forehead like a crack on an egg. "You watch your fucking hands, Bwana Boy," she snarled, hoisting a can of made in the USA, organically grown pepper spray clipped to her rig. She gave the aerosol a little squeeze, enough to make Tonio's eyes water, before returning to her first-class couch like a card shark backing out of a saloon with four shots left in his Smith and Wesson.

A second surge sent the American onto her pack, a helpless turtle. Tonio's head whipped around in time to see the high-speed Russian built hydrofoil fifty meters to starboard dancing over the waves, sending a frothy wake under the Flying Horse as it passed. Built like an amusement park ride for kids to jump on, the blue hovercraft made the trip from Dar to Stone Town, the Zanzibar port city, in thirty minutes, when the Indian Ocean was calm, forty-five minutes in chop.

The Afro-Italian helicopter pilot recalled the December night in 1992 when George Bush sent US troops onto the beaches of Mogadishu, many of them aboard similar, though technologically far superior, flying boats. Addressing the phantom, Tonio muttered, "Me. If I had stayed in the military?

I would have liked to pilot one of those." He glanced in the direction of the American. She had popped her quick release and righted herself minus the bulky load, a tiny woman, Tonio observed, with uncommonly big legs. He winked and mouthed the word, *Fucking*. She gave him the finger and chewed the wrapper off a Power Bar.

"But it was time to leave," Tonio sighed, forced once again to laugh at the irony of events. Soon after the debacle with the U.S. Rangers on October 3, 1993, the Americans pulled out, quick to blame a share of their misery on Italian intelligence provided to Somali warlords. Tonio's sorties quadrupled in number, and being Tonio, the volume of his business grew accordingly. He sold rations, spare parts, fuel, ammunition, boots, anything but food aid, to the clans with the cash, dollars, Deutsche Marks, French Francs, even Italian Lira. He made a killing in a very short time. An alert supply officer caught Tonio red handed in December. To minimize embarrassment, the Italian commander traded a court martial for Tonio's early discharge.

Just after New Year's 1994, a civilian again, Tonio bought an old Land Rover from a Brit in Nairobi, filled it with canned meat, bottled water, cases of beer and set out for Arusha, Tanzania where he was immediately brought on board as a military consultant by US State Department officials conducting peace talks between the majority-Hutu led government of Rwandan President Juvenal Habyarimana and the persistent Tutsi rebels of the Rwandan Patriotic Front. In early April 1994, American diplomats coerced a short-lived power sharing agreement between Habyarimana and the RPF. The President died on the short flight back to Kigali when, by all accounts, his plane was hit by a missile fired from the Rwandan capital by a Hutu extremist, igniting a month-long holocaust. "Lucky for me I found a Tanzanian partner before the Arusha talks ended. Lucky too that I had State Department stationary and a purloined gold foil seal to persuade the Minister of Energy to approve the purchase of my first gold mine."

The late morning sky burned bluer than the sea. Tonio spotted Snake Island, the first in a chain of tiny islands curling off the coral table of Zanzibar like a shrimp tail. Then he saw Stone Town, washed bright white with lime over the coral masonry. Blue and white, blue and white, blue and white, the sky acting like a gigantic palm produced blue and white wind without shade. Tonio's eyes burned worse than when the American woman pissed her pepper in them.

&

Salim-el-Hassan, Minister of Commerce, sent a sand brown Mercedes to gather Tonio at the port. After checking in at Clove House, Tonio commandeered the minister's car for a quick tour of the Swahili town, a concert of tall, skinny, flattop buildings, their doors elaborately carved and fitted with massive hardware, tarnished black brass hinges and hasps that locked fast across stone thresholds. Cool, narrow alleys barely wide enough to accommodate the minister's powerful Mercedes sedan teemed with veiled Muslim women in dark, flowing robes, and thin, rust colored men shrouded in white. With a pilot's skill to remain oriented, Tonio noted the locations of an English pub and a cluster of goldsmiths and gem sellers tucked inside the coral maze. Exiting the old city near the Anglican church built over the site of a pre-colonial slave depot, the minister's driver sped down a deserted boulevard flanked by Soviet inspired housing blocks and government buildings equally totalitarian in spirit, bare concrete darkened by tropical fungus, all of them inappropriate to the scale of Stone Town.

Tonio addressed the phantom with furtive nonchalance. "An armpit, Tony. Like Mogadishu."

The office of the energy minister was housed in a monolith of low ceilings seeming to slip down walls crowded with oppressively tiny windows. A short, dark-skinned woman shaped like a capital S escorted Tonio into Salim-el-Hassan's office suite. He was two hours late and the minister, tired of waiting, had gone out. The S-shaped woman served instant coffee and fussed with a cannibalized air conditioner, its dirty foam filter exposed to the world as the old machine gasped and wheezed and clattered, blowing icy, Freon humid air against the back of Tonio's neck. The minister's red phone, its receiver grimy with use like a dirty necked kid, rested inside a handmade hardwood box fitted with a large padlock. The minister's cheap plastic laminate desktop, designed to imitate oak, spalled off and curled up at all four corners. The unwashed windows, opaque and curtainless, winced with myopia. The coffee was horrible and the brown crystals of unrefined sugar he had scooped into it had failed to dissolve. Tonio had seen worse, but he considered leaving when suddenly a sticky side door to the office popped open with a well-practiced kick.

Tonio snapped to attention. "Excellency! I was beginning to think you had other business!"

Salim-el-Hassan, a huge man, uncomfortable in his heavy, Western suit, laughed heartily, shook Tonio's hand and waved for him to sit on a hideous blue vinyl couch. Salim took a seat in a matching easy chair. "My business is here in Zanzibar, Island of Spices. My driver said you have already toured Stone Town. Good. We are proud of our island, but you must admit, we are poor."

Tonio fished for a bromide. "Poor in gold, Excellency, but rich in culture."

"Culture will not buy a villa in the south of France. Have you considered my proposal, Tonio?"

"Excellency, I already pay customs duties on every gemstone that leaves Tanzania."

"But you pay too much in Europe! I have contacts in Marseilles, as I told you. With my help your goods will reach French soil for next to nothing and then you may trade freely throughout Europe. I ask only that you try my service. If you are not satisfied, pay no tax."

Tonio pretended to consider the offer before announcing, "I have paint."

"Paint?"

"Naval paint, ten thousand gallons U.S. battleship gray."

"Where did you get so much paint?"

Tonio pointed at the window to the sea, a blue splash of the imagination. "Last week, pirates boarded the Louisiana based Cocoa Islander, a freighter carrying forty-five thousand tons of corn, forty thousand grain sacks and ten thousand gallons of paint."

"Ah, the hijacking, yes, I heard. That was the tenth ship this year. But the U.N. High Commissioner in Dar said the bags were taken."

"They were bags conveniently marked with the American AID logo." Tonio flashed a wicked smile. "They can be filled with moldy wheat salvaged from the Argentine ship impounded for weevils last month and sold in the market for the price of corn meal. No, Excellency, I could arrange for the paint to come through the port here for shipment to Marseilles, if we have a deal."

"We have a deal."

"Then I must be going."

"But the Flying Horse won't be returning until mid-morning tomorrow. You must stay, take a spice tour, visit the Slave Cave, enjoy our beautiful climate. There is a shuttle on Sunday as well. Take some time to relax, Tonio."

"I intend to, Excellency, but I prefer to explore the riches unescorted. I hope you don't mind. Monday I will send my associate to finalize the details of our agreement if that is all right with you."

"And the paint?"

"The paint is already here, Excellency," Tonio grinned.

Slowly, the minister's round face wrinkled into a broad smile.

"Tonio, what they say about you is true."

"What do they say, Excellency?"

"They say you have a rock in your stomach, that nothing escapes your notice and therefore nothing surprises you. We will export your paint as plastic soccer balls and you will see that my system works. Then perhaps we will begin to ship gold?"

"Rubies first," Tonio smiled. "I have more rubies than you can imagine, Excellency."

&

On Sunday morning at ten a.m. sharp, a beat-up yellow taxi belching black soot dropped Tonio at the port where a robotic solider waved the hungover Afro-Italian in his blistering red tank top, skintight black pants and copious gold chains to pass through the immigration booth without inspection. The sheer size of the sweltering crowd milling expectantly around the hovercraft berth provoked a disdainful snicker from Tonio. He proceeded gingerly to the end of the pier where the Flying Horse, clean and white, bobbed gently as an inflatable seahorse on the azure waves of a kiddy pool. Tonio had timed his arrival in the hope of boarding immediately to avoid the hot breath of the sun and the second-class passengers. But instead of fawning first class stewards, he was surprised to find several hundred more expectant passengers stranded on the dock, an amorphous queue growing unsteadily, growing like a virus under a microscope.

As travelers continued to attach themselves to the group, Tonio was soon surrounded, submerged, swallowed, forced to surrender to the mob's single purpose of boarding the Flying Horse come hell or high water. His head hurt and he wished he had stuffed a couple of cans of beer into his shoulder bag. "My friend," he whispered to the phantom, "when we get up to the first-class deck, me, I'm buying you a cold one. Make that three!"

"Excuse me?" came an unanticipated response, startling Tonio. The gaunt smuggler wheeled around into the sun rouged face of the long-legged Belgian beauty he had counted as the best-looking first-class woman on Friday's trip over to Zanzibar. "Do you speak English?"

Tonio smiled for the first time since stumbling back to Clove House from Fisherman Pub at midnight. "Perfectly. You?"

63

"*Je crois bien*, yes," laughed the self-absorbed Belgian woman sporting the same sleeveless blue blouse and khaki shorts she had on forty-eight hours earlier. She smelled like raw shrimp and Schnapps.

Tonio had changed clothes a half dozen times, always dousing his face and neck liberally with Bombay aftershave. "Do you know, why aren't we boarding?"

"The Russian hydrofoil is broken since before yesterday. They are trying to comprehend if the Flying Horse can carry so much passengers I think."

"No."

"Yah."

Tonio studied the situation, quickly calculating that the Sunday morning crowd waiting to board the Flying Horse might fill every first- and second-class seat. He began to chew the inside of his lip nervously and pressed forward when suddenly the crowd surged ahead, dragging him with it like a swimmer caught in a swell. The Belgian woman vanished. A few seconds later he elbowed his way into the neck of the funnel and up the gangplank, scrambling past second class doors, climbing the spotless Flying Horse stairs to the spacious, air-conditioned lounge.

The initial chill left Tonio momentarily speechless. He threw himself down on one of the orange, foam filled couches, his eyes darting about in search of a beer seller. A Sikh wearing a white turban smudged with use plopped down hard, his hip pocket brushing the top of Tonio's head. Snapping into an upright position, Tonio mentally protested the invasion of his couch but remained silent when an African man in a brown suit, pink shirt and blue tie descended on the other side with his wife, a very large African woman, and three daughters, pretty, coal black girls wearing crackling crisp white Sunday dresses, each with a clean bow tied at the breast, one red, one yellow and one green.

The air no longer felt cool. Bedraggled passengers continued to stream into the first-class lounge until every couch was filled to capacity. But still passengers boarded. Some sat stiffly upon the tables, others sprawled on the floor as the steady crush of travelers forced them to pull in their arms and legs. Luggage of all sizes, cartons and containers, bags, valises, an occasional backpack like the one attached to the pepper spraying American woman from the trip over, cluttered the no longer spacious aisles. By the time the Flying Horse chugged away from the Stone Town dock, first class carried nearly three hundred passengers and a volume of cargo rarely seen even in bush taxis and buses.

The smile pasted to Tonio's sweating face throbbed as if it had been ironed on. There was no room for beer sellers in first class. "Besides," Tonio reasoned for the benefit of the phantom, "they probably unloaded all the beer and beer sellers to accommodate the riffraff from the hydrofoil. Greedy bastards. You think we would be invited aboard the hydrofoil if the Flying Horse could not sail?"

"Sir?" inquired the African man in the brown suit, pink shirt and blue tie.

"Crowded," groused Tonio.

"Unusually so," the African nodded. "My family and I feel very fortunate to have seats at all. We had tickets for the hovercraft yesterday, but she did not sail. We were forced to spend the night in a dirty guesthouse. Then when she was canceled again this morning, my heart sank you know. We have to be back in Dar tonight to catch our flight to Nairobi. Joseph is my name, sir. I am an architect." The brown man in the brown suit extended his hand. He had a pleasant face.

Even as selfish melancholy swept over him, Tonio shook the man's hand. He could not bring himself to growl at such an agreeable smile. "You'll be back in plenty of time to get to the airport." Tonio had spent much of his life traveling in Africa. He'd experienced far worse than this, brutal mobs rushing airplanes to grab limited seats; government fat cats cutting in the front of long ticket lines, bringing their friends, family and household effects with them; village mamas trying to light charcoal grills while their goats farted in the aisles of passenger aircraft; ferries, trucks, trains, taxies dangerously overloaded;

and wrecks: planes, cars, busses, body parts scattered like rose petals in the middle of nowhere. "I had expected a return trip similar to the trip over. First class was a pleasure on Friday, almost empty, cold beer, beautiful women." Tonio winked, resigning himself to disappointment.

"What a difference a day can make," Joseph replied, "And what do you do, sir?"

"I own a gold mine northeast of Kilimanjaro."

"Gold?"

"Gold, and I export gemstones as well, rubies, sapphires, Tanzanite." Tonio relaxed a bit and fanned himself with the black plastic bag folded and stapled to his first-class ticket, "I know of a plain not far from Ngoro Ngoro where rubies cover the ground like sand on a beach. Can you imagine that? The Japanese are trying to convince the Tanzanian government to turn the whole area into a rice project."

"Rice? Interesting."

"Rice my ass!" Tonio sneered. "The Asians want the rubies."

The architect nodded knowingly. "I see."

The Flying Horse suddenly pitched the passengers to one side then the other then back and back again before the clumsily overloaded catamaran steadied itself. Tonio noticed that passengers were looking at each other like inmates being ferried to a penal colony. "Devil's Island," he muttered for the benefit of the phantom.

A few tense seconds passed and then the Flying Horse began to rock, very subtly at first, side-to-side, bow-to-stern. "Rough seas," tittered Joseph, fussing anxiously with the lapel of his brown suit. "My wife gets seasick."

"She does?" Tonio immediately thought of an air sickness remedy he had administered on more than one occasion and dug through his bag for a bottle of amber aftershave lotion. "Tell her if she feels lightheaded to sniff this." Tonio laughed loudly and looked around for beautiful women. He spotted the Belgian and the pretty Indians in their flowered dresses making the return trip to the mainland. The sky darkened. Waves broke over the twin hulls of the rigid catamaran sending froth against the windows in heavy droplets that smacked the glass like spit. The American woman sat with her backpack against the wall, her eyes pushed against her knees. The dark-blue skinned African woman who had worn the sleeveless Dutch wax wrap on Friday chose a yellow silk sheath which only highlighted her sallow appearance on the ill-fated return trip. The tall Norwegian blond in a sky-blue sun suit sat beneath a wide brimmed straw hat shading, on either side of her, small African boys dressed in dull, dark and threadbare shirts and trousers. Tonio could not suppress a chuckle. Everyone looked petrified. "This chop is nothing!" he snapped to the phantom. "Not to me, chopper pilot."

"No?" Joseph asked with a puzzled expression.

"I've been in aircraft when turbulence is so bad that there is even vomit on the overhead instruments." His eyes met the cloudy yellow and black eyes of Joseph's wife, syrupy chocolate skin cascading in smooth folds over her face, rolling down her thick neck and disappearing into a tent dress covered with portraits of Africa's revolutionary heroes, Julius Nyerere, Jomo Kenyatta, Kenneth Kaunda, Patrice Lumumba, Robert Mugabe and Seko Tore. Milky puke splashed out of her mouth as if an invective she wished she could take back. At the exact same moment, the American woman spit up undigested grains with an agonized wail and across the deck an Indian girl wearing an expensive red sari trimmed in real gold, a white flower laced into her jet black hair, vomited breakfast. Tonio could smell cumin and tamarind.

The Flying Horse bucked. For a protracted instant not one passenger moved. Tonio was reminded of a training flight in a DC-3 that his instructor crash landed near Milan, shearing off the landing gear as the giant twin props chewed through a field, setting fire to acres of tall grass. That's what three women puking at once felt like, helplessness in the presence of obstinate fate. The Indian girl started to cry. The American groaned. Joseph's wife said, "I feel better now." A good-looking young man traveling with the Belgian woman puked.

Tonio knew that once one man let go of his lunch others would quickly follow. Less than a minute after Joseph's wife threw up, thirty passengers, maybe more, men, women, boys, girls, had lost their cookies. Only then did two stewards from the Flying Horse appear with big boxes of black plastic *Flying Horse Ship Sickness Bags.* During the next sixty seconds, another fifty passengers chucked their fortunes into quart size sacks. The Norwegian blond filled two. The American woman kept spitting into hers. The proud Sikh held his turban with one hand, drooling into the Flying Horse seasick bag held in his other hand. Five minutes after Joseph's wife started the rash of hysterical puking, fully fifty percent of the three hundred passengers jammed into first class held clammy bags over their mouths, most of them retching and groaning, their faces Toulouse Lautrec green, their eyes as red as enraged monsters. The lounge smelled like a sewer. All three of Joseph's pretty daughters puked, causing Joseph's wife to puke again and again. The beautiful Indian woman in the flowered dress sat in a puddle of sticky goo that looked like brownie mix. The African beauty coughed and hacked and spat watery nothing directly onto the carpet. By the time another five minutes had passed, seventy-five percent of the passengers retched into black bags, which were fast growing scarce since both first-class stewards were sidelined by seasickness too.

Tonio struggled to look at no one. He breathed slowly in an attempt to filter out any fumes that might upset his steely control of the situation. He peered out the windows, methodically scanning the horizon in every direction, but all he could see was the unpredictable Indian Ocean, a treacherously agitated, priceless blue jewel.

"Talk to me, Joseph!" he barked. "Look at me, not at your wife. She will be all right as soon as we get to Dar. What do you build? Houses?"

Joseph looked petrified. He shook his head "No," then puked all over Tonio's Gucci loafers before the gold miner could rip the seasick bag from his ticket and paste it over the architect's mouth.

Thirty minutes into the voyage everyone in the first-class lounge so far as Tonio could see was either puking or had puked and now moaned and groaned green gilled into a puke bag. He tried to focus on the phantom who had helped him through every childhood nightmare, every racial taunt when he attended the French School in Kinshasa as a boy, every awkward moment as an adolescent with dreams of becoming the first Afro-Italian astronaut, every test and trial in college and the military. "I bet it's twice as bad on the lower deck," he whispered. "We have a first-class ticket and we have been through worse without vomiting ever!"

Across the lounge, Tonio spied the Belgian beauty as she looked up from caressing the sweat streaked hair of her companions, two puking men and one blubbering, gagging woman. Her face flushed, coquettish strands of raven hair glued to her sweaty forehead, Tonio could see that she had not given herself over to mass hysterical seasickness. He smiled. She smiled back. He felt a tremendous bond had just been forged with a dreamy woman possessing fortitude second only to his own.

For the next hour, the two of them sat apart ten meters, their toes in a turgid sea of vomit thick with wailing, retching seal pups, staring into each other's eyes. The heat was truly unpleasant, the air fouler than a Mogadishu latrine. The Flying Horse hobbled slowly, slowly across the strait from Zanzibar to Dar es Salaam. Tonio fantasized that the Belgian woman fantasized about him. After ninety minutes, the length of a normal trip on the Flying Horse, the continent of Africa was just barely visible when the waves parted. After two hours, most of the crying and moaning had degenerated into self-pitying whimpers. The first-class lounge on the Flying Horse resembled a mausoleum filled with unhappy, undead souls, except for two, Tonio and the Belgian beauty.

"Make that three," boasted the phantom as the Flying Horse trotted across the chop past the Cocoa Islander, the ship Tonio's pirates had raided by shinnying up the anchor chain a few days earlier. Tonio smiled at the Belgian woman, imagining they would have dinner together that night at Casanova's out on the exotic Msasani Peninsula near Tanzania's secret defensive missile batteries. As if in agreement, she smiled back. Then, for the first time in two hours and fifteen long minutes, the captain cut power to the Flying Horse's engines and the catamaran lurched like a stomach full of water. A few passengers puked anew but most only retched and groaned, a sick man rolling off a stretcher face down in the muck. The Belgian woman's eyes lit up then just as quickly paled. She pouted seductively and hurled shrimp curdled in Schnapps all over the heads of her companions triggering another round of hysterical vomiting from the downright disgusting group.

Tonio looked deep into the eyes of the phantom who looked askance and puked between his skinny knees. The smuggler had never felt so alone. He sat there alone, the one person aboard the Flying Horse who had not puked, a pariah, an arrogant winner perched on a pedestal built for one and only one. Tonio, macho and sad, felt hot and humiliated by his own determination never to give in, never to step one foot outside the imaginary world of first class on the Flying Horse. When the limping catamaran bumped the dock in Dar es Salaam, all the doors flew open. While others sponged puke from their clothes with napkins, handkerchiefs, their bare hands even, Tonio made sure his red tank top was tucked in neatly and he walked, back straight, head high, but humbled, his phantom beaten to the gangplank. First one off the Flying Horse, sad. Tonio's Gucci loafers and the blue veined ankles of his sockless feet were splattered with everyone else's wretched vomit.

4. George's Dream

The instant Lenny died, so did George's dream of land of his own, a shank of black soil good for growing tomatoes and beans, and a fishing pond or maybe a lazy trout stream rippling through a small green woods ripe with deer and fat rabbits and raspberries.

Build himself a little cedar log cabin with a door only he had the key to, and a bed sawed with his own two hands, a clean blanket, a new pillow too to lay his head down on and dream about rabbit stew and juicy peach pie.

Bluest sky ever imagined, the sweetest wind, and real quiet. Never again hungry and never again afeared to look the boss right in the eye because the boss that looked back at him, in George's dream, was a shiny, clean-shaven image in a fancy oval mirror.

George left Salinas, took to drinking, couldn't keep a job when he found one. Wasn't long before no boss anywhere would give him work over the next bum in line who at least could stand up straight. Started stealing just to eat. Folks watched him with suspicion. And if they caught him taking something of theirs, why they'd give him a good whipping and run him out of town.

When the rains got so bad the valley flooded, the orphan boy who George gave his last bruised apple to literally carried the sunken farm worker to high ground, to an old gray barn that offered little protection from chill winds, but at least it kept them dry. Then that there family showed up. The boy didn't know whether to hurry and hide in the loft or escape back into the rain, but he knew he couldn't leave George alone, dying from hunger like he was.

But as the old ma approached, the scared boy leapt up and cried, "Help me help him. Man's astarvin.' Tried feeding him rain, but he can't swaller." And the Ma took the boy with her, and she led everyone but Rose of Sharon outside to sit under the overhang for a spell.

George choked on his last breath dreaming about his mother, the smell of her breast, the gentle murmur of blood moving inside her, the shudder of white light while he slowly drown in warm milk. And with an arcing spasm, like a man thrown headfirst into a deep gorge, did poor George die.

Rose of Sharon couldn't tell the difference between the smell of death and the smell of that old whispering barn, not after clutching her blue stillborn for a day and a night until Pa could make a little coffin out of an orange crate and Ma made her bury it.

She sat a piece watching George twitch, listening. Then she hoisted her tired body up and drew the comforter about her. She moved slowly to the corner and stood looking down at the wasted face, into those wide, frightened eyes. Then slowly she lay down beside him. He shook his head slowly from side to side. Rose of Sharon loosened one side of the blanket and bared her breast. "You got to," she said. She squirmed closer and pulled his head close. "There!" she said. "There." Her hand moved behind his head and supported it. Her fingers moved gently in his hair. She looked up and across the barn, and her lips came together and smiled mysteriously.

5. THE RACCOON

H appened in Amish country up on Oak Hill at the end of the rocky lane, that big old white house looking down at muddy North Fork.

My dogs, from the time I got up that morning, they were acting nervous, scrabbling around on the porch grab three-or-four bits of dry food from a big blue bowl by the kitchen screen door. I poured myself a cup of coffee and filled the work Thermos. My three 40-pound mutts colored jet black, red ale and towhead crunched food, chattered across weathered floorboards, their toenails, long from the muddy spring, noisy as children playing with dice. Down the front steps they trouped, and across the yard to an old willow tree splayed by lightning beside the red toolshed.

Overnight chill clinging to unwashed windows already felt warm when I pushed my face against cracked panes to watch my dogs one-at-a-time poke their noses under that shaggy willow, then lurch backward. They each did this a few times before packing back to the porch for more food, loud chewing, and the clack-clack of black toenails.

Forgetting the dogs for a minute, I shoved a dark bread sandwich into my wrinkled lunch sack and sipped steaming coffee cooling with the slow certainty that by noon my cheddar cheese slices would soften to the contours of thick-sliced summer sausage. It would be a hot day, good for framing roofs.

Again, I heard the dogs murmuring outside, their heavy ceramic food bowl bumping against an old round porch column. "What?" I finally shouted. Three grinning dogs pushed their rubber noses against the rusting backdoor screen, hips waggling, tails aswing like skipping ropes. "Something botherin' you out there?"

To the east, a cool row of pines separated the uncombed willow from old farmer Joe's plow-blackened soy field grown dusty green with bean sprouts. Underneath branches spraying gracefully up-then-down-again like water from a hose lay the raccoon.

For a spooky second, I feared the dogs had really found a young child, so big was the raccoon, and lying on its back, spread-eagled like that, or a child's broken horse. Then I relaxed, believing it dead, and whistled my dogs to back off, give me space to kneel in red pine needles and worm beneath willow whips still prickly with spring buds.

If dead, it was fresh-dead, the raccoon on the bed of half-frozen humus, sickeningly warm, its blood crimson, its muscles visibly stiffened. The dogs bumped into each other and nipped at the frayed blue pockets of my faded work jeans. Should they dive on the raccoon, they wanted to know, tear it up and toss its parts about like an old chew toy? What should they do? The raccoon excited them. Could they have it? Please?

I slithered close, afraid the dead raccoon might jump me awake, claw off my nose before ripping out the eyes of the dogs who had first disturbed its slumber. It's big, and surely would be a fierce coon upon a dog were its belly not sliced open. But not shot, that I could tell, lying there on its back begging the question dogs never ask—Why? It was still bleeding. Gravity struggled to pull its paws into the ground.

The dogs whimpered and tried to crawl under the tree with me and the raccoon in the winter shade, a south wind draping branches like a damp dishrag. My eyes giant telescopes, I gazed back in time to watch the rabid claws of coonhound ripping through broomthick coonfur, a frantic coon hunter clubbing, kicking to get the raccoon off his dog. Gravely wounded, the raccoon must have made its way through thick timber lining ravines clear down to South Fork to get up here and die under my willow.

Is it alive? Have my dogs not dragged it around the yard while I am making lunch because the raccoon has hissed them like a snake, swiped at their noses, a compromise to wrastle dogs no more in exchange for not ending up a spilt bag of broken bones in the jaws of dog?

There was no movement of the ribcage, but I felt raccoon breath and laughed nervously like a dog unable to resist poking its nose against the backdoor screen. Supporting myself on one elbow, I tried to touch the back of the black-clawed paw nearest me when suddenly up sat the raccoon, grabbing two of my fingers. The pressure of five steel-sharpened awls eased up just before breaking my skin. Walnut raccoon eyes and its bloody grimace promised to rip out my throat if I moved any closer. I felt hot wind not breath, and the coon stiffened its spine above the belly wound, and its eyes filled with purple ink.

This really impressed my dogs. They moved in close to smell the marvelous conjunction of life and death as the raccoon released my fingers, its beautiful mask relaxed from predator to resemble cartoon again. Menace dissolving at my fingertips, the raccoon sighed, lay back down and yielded to betrayal by dogs.

Or if it was the size of a rabbit, I think, like the rabbit I killed after the dogs mangled it, I could easily kill the raccoon, a soft, warm rabbit under a coarse burlap sack, under my calloused hand, a rabbit no longer afraid of dogs. And smashed the rabbit's skull with a hickory stick two inches thick. And the breath of the rabbit moved up the stick into my muscles, the shimmering final animal pang quickly gone. In a hot fire, in the rusted trash barrel where I had often thrown dead birds and slow squirrels, I burned the burlap sack with the rabbit inside, lavender flames joyfully consuming fur and bone the way teething dogs chew and chew and chew.

So, I ran my dogs down to the old keeled-over corncrib and rousted sleeping, straw-colored cats to fetch another burlap sack, and I ran back and tried to cover over the raccoon. Unsure, I knelt under the tree holding a length of galvanized drainpipe. Or a rock. Or a knife. Or a bow and arrow. Or if you were the sun and hurled down a meteor to smash the raccoon dead. But the raccoon grabbed my sack and pulled me closer. The dogs sprang backward. The raccoon grumbled low, bared its rusted teeth, its tongue a dusty road. Never would it hide under a grass bag while I smashed its head, not while strength remained in its paws to tear off my hand and eat it in front of me, then kill the dogs and eat them too. And let go the sack, and me. And fell back to earth beneath the willow. And deflated flat except for the meager crown of its ribs.

Well, I had a big, heavy kettle, which I lugged under the tree and tipped carefully over the raccoon. Off to work I drove knowing my dogs, even if they tried, could not bother the poor beast buried beneath the pot. That day one of the other carpenters showed up at the job with a bale of frozen coonskins that he peeled apart and spread out on a gravel pile to thaw. A fur buyer came by at lunch and paid 900-dollars for the raccoon pelts. Now I already knew from countless lunch hour tales that this carpenter was a diehard coon hunter. I'd seen his hunting outfit, oversized pants and shirt stiff with rancid coongrease, his shotguns, Willie and Waylon, his illegal spotlights. He had three dogs of his own, expensive Blue Tick hounds.

Turns out, after work the very night before, he was out coon hunting along the river when his 1200-dollar coonhound Duke treed a hugely-monstrous coon, and before he could shoot that coon that coon come down that damn o'cottonwood and commenced to fightin' with o'Duke and looked like o'Duke might even win when that o'coon jumps up and grabs o'Duke by the back of the neck and starts shakin' him so hard o'Duke's ears was flappin' and would have bit clean through the dog's spine except my other two-worthless-one-thousand-and-two-hundred-dollars-coonhounds finally shows up and scares that coon away. But don't even bother to shoot that worthless coon, its fur's all chewed up and ain't no good to nobody now. But don't have no choice but to shoot o'Duke, so tore up he is he ain't worth savin' even.

One muggy, end of summer day, my dogs peacefully snoozing on the cool gray planks of the shaded porch, old farmer Joe's bean field already yellowing, the strawberry-blond willow drooping with thirst, ground underneath brittle as an old tombstone, I lifted the heavy pot to reveal an exact circle of pure black stink, a portrait of raccoon death, its anonymous stain leeching deep into the roots where once the raccoon held me by the claw.

6. LILY JO

A woman with long platinum hair wearing armfuls of expensive bling surfaced out of a tall-backed booth tucked into the side room at the Java Shoppe, crawled to the head of the line of mid-morning customers, and with an annoying whisper, interrupted the new barista who was plenty busy already taking orders, "Joan, Nile decaf when you have a sec?"

The new barista, a striking young woman with blue and orange highlights in her artfully disordered dark hair, stopped just as Oisín was about to order, robotically shuffled over to a row of coffee pots, carried one of them into the side room, and curled her upper lip into a public sneer when she refilled the woman's coffee bean brown cup.

Moving in painful slow motion, the barista returned to the "Place Order" end of the counter facing the blackboard with all the coffees and sizes and prices for muffins and cookies, the whole menu written in colored chalk, smudged, erased, and overwritten to the point of illegibility.

Her face expressionless, she said, "Sorry to keep you waiting, sir. What can I get you?"

Oisín replied pleasantly, "Large dark roast to go, please, Joan."

She entered his order into a credit card reader. "Got a name?"

"In fact, I do. It's Oisín." The much-older man studied the much-younger woman's right arm, a sleeve of green and red tattoo ink covering otherwise fair skin beginning at the enameled medical alert around her wrist and disappearing over her shoulder. "That's quite an intricate tattoo, Joan. Must be a mighty interesting story behind all that imagery."

"I'm a mighty interesting story, all right," Joan replied dryly; "a Wikipedia of medical miracles." She studied Oisín's eyes, his streaked with grey like his hair. Her eyes, Oisín observed from a stolen glance into them, reminded him of wet cedar boards.

Saturday morning, the end of the new barista's first week working at the Java Shoppe, Oisín arrived right at opening, six a.m., a teardrop bag slung over his right shoulder, as usual. His car idled at the curb outside, warming up on a chilly October morning, to carry him up Highway 61 along the Mississippi to a book launch in Red Wing. "Gonna be a beautiful day today for a drive along the great river from the looks of it, Joan."

"Hang on a sec, ok?" Joan hurried through the small café switching on lights and window signs before returning to the counter. "Looks nice out, but I'm stuck in here till we close at one. Having the dark roast to go this morning, Ocean?"

"Yes, thank you, Joan. Make it a Rio Grande." His bearded face morphed an avuncular smile hoping to dodge her lurking mercurial behavior with a compliment. "You must be fitting in well here; opening up for the boss."

"Only so Kim can sleep in." Joan shook her head, her hair pulled back into a long, multicolored ponytail as wild as any mare's, her eyebrows taut with appealing innocence. "She's always shorthanded. Practically begged my stepmom to get me to apply to work here."

Before the new barista could turn away, Oisín said, "Say, I wanted to show you this …" He fished a stainless-steel medical necklace from inside his hooded, light blue pullover. "… I wear a Staff of Asclepius necklace. I see you have the bracelet."

"Ahh." She drew out the word, feinting interest in Oisín's prattle. "Mm-huh."

Oisín mused before continuing: *Joan must be twenty. Barely, if. Maybe eighteen; a high school senior.* He wanted to ask her age but, leery of generational sarcasm, or of himself appearing creepy, he did not. Instead, he offered bits of unsolicited information. "Asclepius, the original owner of the staff you see here, was a Greek physician. He had two daughters, Hygeia, the goddess of health, and Panacea, goddess of healing."

Joan replied, "Let me guess, the daughters would be hygiene and snake oil."

"Panacea isn't exactly snake oil ..." Oisín muttered.

"Sugar pills and fiddle sticks," grumbled Joan, her eyes darkening. She continued unprompted, "I've tried 'em all, Mr. Ocean, and I've had a dozen panacea surgeries. So please don't tell me about snake oil. Surgeons have slathered it into both my heart chambers, and my heart is still cheddar-cheesed with tiny holes."

"I'm sorry to hear that. If I may ask: you have a septal defect?"

"Septal defectsssss," Joan hissed, "atrial and ventricular septal birth defects to be exact. You're not a cardiologist?"

"Patient." Oisín jiggled his necklace. "A patient patient, Joan, that's me. Double Ps—patience and peace. They keep me alive."

"Bad heart?"

"No heart." Oisín hoisted his Patagonia teardrop. "Well, here's my heart."

"Heart in a bag?" Joan laughed, amused, "Forget the sugar pills, sweetie, you need a new heart. I'm on the list, but I might as well be like ten billion down. Occasionally my name inches up because I'm having a critical episode, but there's no donors because I'm AB negative, so I'm hard to match. Meanwhile, growing up, my heart size kept changing too. Now, I have lupus. Not in my karma to get a heart. I must have been a rattlesnake or something awful in my past life."

"No, no, no. Don't think like that." Oisín avoided Lily Jo's eyes. "I've never been listed."

Lily Jo wagged her finger. "I'd get right on that if I were you."

"Yeah," he chuckled. "Long story short, I had a heart attack; my left heart imploded; my kidneys went sideways during surgery to place this LVAD to take over pumping my blood."

Oisín half-unzipped his silver-grey shoulder bag containing batteries and a controller connected to a pump below his heart via a quarter inch silicone sheathed power and data cable passing through his abdomen. "Transplant screeners told me they couldn't do double organ transplants because there were too few donors in this region." Oisín forced a stupid grin he immediately regretted because he was not looking for pity, but rather someone to talk to.

Joan looked at him with an expression of disappointment. "So, why don't you go sit down, I'll make coffee and call you when it's ready."

The old fellow moved to a storefront stool. With her back to him, Lily Jo prepared coffee, a solemn, time-consuming morning ritual at the Java Shoppe. She swayed, her hips going one way, her shoulders the other, the hem of her silky dress brushing the smooth backs of her knees. He caught himself staring, twitched his head and picked up a book from the storefront coffee table, a serious-looking tome of his own short stories published two decades earlier.

"Oceans of Loam and Ice" it was called, though he couldn't immediately remember the table of contents. It wasn't an imposingly fat book, but a hard back complete with a frayed dustcover, a postage-stamp black and white portrait of him on the back taken outside a North Shore cabin on this fiftieth birthday twenty years earlier. *God, I look so fucking healthy.*

Oisín knew the Java Shoppe owners from the years he'd spent as chairman of the town's economic development commission. They were devout, born-again Christian couple named Kim and Larry, who took out an economic development loan to start a coffee business after the great flood of 2007. Oisín took unusual solace knowing that neither Kim nor Larry had read any of his donated reading materials, his books and issues of his literary magazine, because there were fucks and shits and goddamn sonsofbitches or worse at least once somewhere between every cover, hidden cockroaches riding in a shipment of Walmart toilet paper. His award-winning covers had not been banned at the Java Shoppe, even after they were removed from the high school and public libraries once the head of the city library board, Heidi Carlson, took the time to read them.

"Mr. Ocean!" Lily Jo barked a few minutes later. "Rio Grande dark roast."

Oisín pushed up his glasses and as fast as he could got off the bench. He felt momentarily dizzy, steadied himself a second, and took a few weightless, wobbly steps to reach the end of the counter, which he promptly grabbed.

"For heaven's sake," she scolded him pleasantly. "When are you going to stop calling me Joan?"

"You're not Joan?" Oisín replied.

"I'm Lily Jo, Mr. Ocean."

Oisín ignored what he considered to be a childish pout verging on insouciance. "You go by Jo though, correct?"

"No, sugar pills. I go by Lily Jo." She dipped onto her left elbow, her neck craning toward the blackboard, and pulled up the collar of her wildly colorful dress to expose the back of her left shoulder, a small tattoo woven-in among warren of tats slathering her left arm. It was a lily of the valley, green leaves, small ivory bells, their flairs crimped, dangling from slender green hooks, so perfect in detail Oisín could almost smell the tiny flowers. "Lily Jo," she repeated.

Oisín nodded, a little embarrassed by Lily Jo's lack of inhibition and view of her vertebrae. "Lilies of the valley were my father's favorite," he confessed, "I think because of their intoxicating smell."

"Intoxicating? They do smell pretty, but I'm more addicted to the smell of coffee brewing."

Oisín looked into her eyes for a clue to Lily Jo's charm. "Well then, pet, my name is Mr. Avon. Patrick Oisín Daniel Avon."

"Oh. Well, I think Ocean is an unusual middle name though, isn't it?"

"My middle name, which is the name I've gone by for fifty years or so since I studied one semester in Dublin in college, is Oisín." He spelled it out and wrote it out on Lily Jo's note pad, diacritical and all: "O i s í n. It's Irish. My namesake was the greatest Irish poet in antiquity. Yeats wrote about him an apt epigraph for me:

> *You who are bent, and bald, and blind,*
> *With a heavy heart and a wandering mind,*
> *Have known three centuries, poets sing,*
> *Of dalliance with a demon thing.*

"Oh my gosh," gasped Lily Jo, her eyes expressing the surprise of someone who's tasted hot sauce on eggs for the first time. "I know what dalliance means."

"Me too, Lily Jo. Oh, that's a much prettier name than Joan."

"So did you? Dally with a demon thing?"

"I don't remember exactly, but when I landed, I turned three hundred years old in a last gasp, doomed to carry my dead young man's heart in a bag."

Lily Jo looked into Oisín's eyes, rubbed the back of his shoulder with one hand, like nurses often did, and squeezed the old man's bruised left hand with her other. "But you're still here."

Oisín smiled with the joy of a dying man. He liked Lily Jo and did not try to hide it.

The Java Shoppe closed every Monday, so the following Tuesday, Oisín stopped for coffee at his usual midmorning time. Lily Jo was not there. She wasn't there on Wednesday either. Thursday morning, Kim, the owner, took Oisín's coffee order. "What happened to the new girl?" he asked, quickly correcting himself, "the young woman, Lily Jo."

"She left to seek fortune, fame, and forgiveness, I guess," Kim flippantly replied.

Kim's daughter Marcy mashed sandwiches in a waffle press. "Mom, she said she had to find her place in the world."

"Whatever." Kim turned her back to the counter. "She quit and now we're short-handed again."

Wearing a frock and a white bib apron, Marcy brought over Oisín's coffee after delivering a breakfast sandwich to another patron. "Here you go, Oisín. Careful, it's hot."

"Thank you, Marcy."

"Lily Jo has lots of problems," Marcy whispered, pointing at her forehead.

"Mental?"

Marcy nodded Yes. "More medical than mental."

"I saw she wears a medical alert bracelet."

"She was born with holes in her heart."

"No. Wow."

"She seems pretty normal now; I mean I know she's sick; she's really smart."

Marcy's mother Kim chimed in, "I'm sorry, but she's a heartsick dummy as far as I'm concerned."

"I'm sorry too." Oisín started for the door then turned back. "She's from here, though?"

Marcy whispered again, "She went to middle school here then started high school at Rochester Mayo but came back and finished her senior year in town; we graduated in the same class. She lived off-and-on with her father who's the middle school principal, Marlen Rush. Mr. Rush is married to Jami Dahl, Jami Rush now. Lily Jo doesn't get along with her stepmom, which is why all the moving, plus her heart. She goes to Mayo Clinic for that. But then she got pregnant by the senior class prom king, Freyr Bjarne, and went back to live with her real mom in Rochester right after graduation before moving up to the Cities to go to the U."

"Lily Jo went to the U? And she has a baby?"

Marcy's eyes widened then shrank to fiendish dots. "Neuuuwa. That's why she moved away. My mom says she's going through a living hell of her own doing. That's probably true, but nobody's perfect. She's got a bad heart and no baby. I feel sorry for Lily Jo. I pray for her all the time."

"You think she went to find herself up in the Cities?"

"Who knows? Personally, I think Lily Jo just wants to get away from everything, especially this town and the state of Minnesota. Can't really blame her."

Oisín felt uncomfortable talking about Lily Jo in her absence. "Imagine that," he said. "Well, have a wonderful day, Marcy. Kim."

Patrick Oisín Daniel Avon moved to the southeast corner of Minnesota bordered by Iowa and the Mississippi River after moving from the suburbs of Northern Virginia two decades earlier. He, his wife Florence, his dogs and cat chose to start their lives over in a small rural town dwarfed by bluffs carpeted with hardwood forests, cattle paddocks, and vast agricultural fields. A bucolic landscape indeed—two large, underpopulated counties cleaved by broad, storybook valleys and dark rivers prone to flash flooding. Swift trout stream seams stitched an undulating quilt of corn and soybean fields rimmed by ice age limestone carved when glaciers melted before the gigantic ice sheets were able to grind them down like the rest of the prairies and great plains.

The Driftless Area, enigmatic karst, underground rivers and bat caves, provided near-endless sensory inspiration for Oisín's prose and poetry. But isolated farm towns, the irrepressibly insular, homogeneously white populations inspired his desire to document the slow, steady decline of the rural Upper Midwest, its residents trapped caustically between their disremembered colonial past and an uncertain future. Not two centuries earlier, Dakota Sioux in the Driftless and throughout Minnesota were violently banished to reservations and their lands settled by European pioneers. Oisín had encountered tribes in the remote heart of Africa faced with the exact same historical dilemma imposed by colonial militias. What he experienced when he arrived from inside the Beltway left him curious but empty inside. Socially isolated in rural Minnesota after twenty years of community engagement elsewhere, for the first time in his life Oisín felt unwelcome.

The question he had asked of Marcy, "Is she—Lily Jo—is she from *here?*" was loaded with leaden intent. Oisín quickly learned that he was not from *"here"* despite being born and raised in the Midwest. A man running the asphalt crew that paved Oisín's long driveway, said to him, "When I was eating lunch down at the Norsk Café a guy told me that you were in the second tower of the World Trade Center when it got hit. I mean, man, oh-fucking man. What was that like anyway if you don't mind me asking?"

Oisín had heard similar fabulous rumors of his origin before, but never the World Trade Center fabrication. He and his wife Florence had transplanted themselves from North Arlington, Virginia, fifteen months before 9/11. They both left careers in international development and disaster assistance to start over in a town of 1,500 residents. Florence and Oisín interested townsfolk because they were new, and not "from *here,*" but what interested everyone even more was the dilapidated, once majestic 150-year-old house they had bought and immediately started refurbishing. Locals figured the mysterious city slickers from out east were idiots for buying the Arendahl House. Behind Oisín's back they laughed at him and gossiped.

Having not received the memo that he was an idiot, Oisín set to removing Arborvitae that surrounded and eventually swallowed the house with his chainsaw. Folks passing the Arendahl House every day on the highway still known fondly as "Arendahl Avenue," unanimously agreed that the place looked better once the trees were down.

Oisín and Florence reconstructed the exterior of that old house starting with the 1856 limestone foundation, laid up without mortar, ending with the roof, by hand, by themselves, the aforementioned asphalt crew being one of very few contractors with large machines invited to their project.

Not once did Oisín set foot in the old Norsk Café, knowing he simply lacked the stamina required to take an uninvited seat at the infamous, sixteen chair *Table of Wisdom* and speak the local dialect for more than a grunt or two. Florence, who grew up in a small Iowa town of 500 residents told him he was being a snob. Oisín did not disagree. He was the first to admit he was a snob.

"Artists are always snobs. They have to be. Style and voice and taste are all about snobbery," he liked to point out.

To satisfy he need to articulate his peculiar situation of being secretly watched while publicly ignored, Oisín began writing features for the weekly county newspaper. He started a blog covering rural politics and rural economy hoping that the focus on his adopted region would distract him from writing frustratingly drab fiction that sounded like a decades-long trip report of his years in Africa and inside the Washington Beltway.

In the summer of 2007, after eighteen inches of rain fell one Saturday in August, Oisín's adopted town of Bergen Creek flooded. That fateful evening, the local volunteer fire department and public works posted spotters on the bridges and levee berms ringing the center of town comprised of low-lying business and residential neighborhoods. Flood-watchers stood vigil in the drizzle watching the swollen Root River that ran to the south of city limits, as well Bergen Creek, a popular trout stream that cut through the center of town on its way to dump into the river just east. Fearing the larger Root River might breach the levee, public workers closed the gates, which allowed small floods to rise inside the levee in holding ponds. Around 2 a.m., Bergen Creek suddenly rose, breached the levee system, and filled the town like a bathtub. With the flood relief gates closed against the river, floodwaters just kept rising until 90 downtown businesses and 350 residential structures were inundated.

Well before the sun came up, Oisín slipped on his five-buckle concrete boots and waded past police lines with a camera and press pass on a lanyard around his neck. He went straight to City Hall, which happened to sit above the flood on a knoll so that only the basement suffered damage. He spoke briefly to the Mayor and the County Sheriff, who led the command post. He assured them that he was going to explore the flooded areas.

"Promise I'll be careful."

The mayor started to object, but the Sheriff, whom Oisín had interviewed for other stories, said, "Go ahead. Keep out of trouble, ok?"

When a deputy from one of the adjacent counties spotted Oisín taking photos of damaged homes from the northside bridge over the creek that had caused the flood, the deputy raced up in a brown cruiser, slammed on the brakes for maximum effect, and hopped out of the car red in the face and madder'n the dickens. "Whad-dada-hell you think you're doing?"

Oisín flashed his press ID and took a picture, with flash, of the deputy. "Taking pictures," he said smartly.

"Well, you just take your pictures and march on down the highway north and don't come back this way."

"I'm a reporter. The Sheriff knows I'm out here. He said it was ok."

"I don't care who okayed it. You don't belong out here."

The deputy pointed north. "Now I said get moving."

Oisín pointed southwest. "I live over past City Hall on 33."

"Well, that's just tough shit, sir. I said move it!"

Oisín clenched his teeth, tensed his arms and torso, and started walking. The deputy rolled past on the way back to the northside checkpoint. Oisín sprinted down the first side street to the east past muck covered tennis courts into a hard-hit neighborhood that sprawled along the levee where a veritable tidal wave had come over.

The air was thick with the smell of lawn fertilizer and gasoline. Many of buildings teetered off their foundations; some of the older block and stone foundations had completely collapsed. A couple of natural gas fires burned. One house had exploded, windows shattered black and smouldering with a sick blue-green glow. Streets had buckled. Mud-covered cars sat in water up to their door handles. In the distance, where water rose highest on low-lying streets, rescue teams in canoes and flat boats moved methodically from house-to-house using spotlights to search for stranded inhabitants. A couple of blocks south, a rescue crew had torn a hole in the roof of an assisted living apartment building and were still in the process of rescuing residents, hoisting them onto the shingles and down into a DNR fan boat. Despite the poor lighting, Oisín captured everything he could on film instead of trying to scribble notes; notes he kept in his head.

About the time he was ready to hike back to City Hall—since he'd talked himself out of wading over his boot tops into the lowest areas of the neighborhood—the same damn deputy who chastised him on the northside bridge came racing down the street, engine roaring, lights flashing, throwing mud in his wake. Oisín quickly slogged into water up to his knees, soaking his shoes, wetting the hem of his shorts; he pulled himself onto a porch deck keeled over on the back of a dirty blue house slung cockeyed on its broken block foundation. Through the patio door in back, he spotted a young girl of maybe 8 or 9 sitting on a breakfast counter, knees pulled tight to her chin, a potted plant at her bare feet. Water inside the tilted kitchen covered the stove.

Their eyes made contact in the cloudy pre-dawn grey of disaster. "Help," she whispered.

Oisín wrestled open the patio door warped by the havoc of the flood. "Are you hurt?" he whispered, because the girl had whispered.

"No."

"Is anyone else with you?"

"The creek."

"It's ok," he said. "I've got you now. Let's get you out of this water." Oisín lifted the girl off the counter and carried her outside where the angry deputy waited, a look of bewilderment stitched to his face. "Can you take this girl to the shelter, deputy?" Oisín asked.

"You bet cha," he replied, scrambling to open the backdoor. Oisín waded out of the murky house with the girl in his arms, hers wound tightly around his shoulders, her cheek against his ear. When he tried to set her in the sheriff's cruiser, she clung on.

"Can you take me?" she whispered. "My stepmom didn't come home last night."

"Where's your father?" Oisín whispered.

"I don't know."

Oisín looked into the deputy's suddenly sad blue eyes. "Hop in," said the deputy, his voice betraying no anger. "I'll run you both to the shelter. Not safe around here." The deputy whispered to Oisín, "When she's settled in, you can come back out to take more pictures in the daylight. Be a lot safer for you."

In 2010, Oisín was elected president of the local Economic Development Authority, flush to overflowing with flood reconstruction and new business funding. To Oisín, after years of isolation, the new friendships on the EDA and in the business community—unfulfilling but genuine—seemed a major social breakthrough so long as he kept his expectations simple and low. Saying hello on the street. Being called by and addressing residents by name. First names. Sharing moments of laughter. Gossiping.

Gossip came naturally to the journalist and interviewer who understood its importance as a communication tool. People joining in a discussion of someone who was not present to endorse or refute the storytelling about them revealed more about the gossipers than it did the gossipees. Oisín began to feel he understood the town, the language, and the people who had gossiped so much about him before they had even met him.

Pretty soon, Oisín was pulled in a hundred different directions. His writing suddenly took off, and not just the journalism that gave him a pretext to interview governors, senators and representatives, presidential hopefuls, government leaders, business leaders, local leaders from all over the state, as well as hundreds of ordinary people who always populated his stories, but his fiction as well. He sold a short story after a long dry spell, and his poems were suddenly being accepted by literary magazines. Then a publisher accepted Oisín's third novel-length manuscript, "Neuf Paroles Triste." The book sold poorly, but that didn't slow down the growth of his local celebrity. Oisín, journalist, author, man with the mysterious past, became the subject of stories, interviews, photo shoots, television, and YouTube videos.

Just ahead of the tenth anniversary of the great 2007 flood, Oisín woke one hot July morning with a monster inside his chest. He survived a massive myocardial infarction that morning, but he lived, and died, through another half-dozen aftershocks the following week whenever his heart stopped dead and he had to be revived with countershocks. Cardiologists at Mayo clinic implanted a pacemaker. When that didn't stop his minutes-long visits to the edge of the sensory black abyss where time stood still, cardiologists implanted a defibrillator. The defibrillator pre-empted knock-knock-knocking on heaven's door, but it did not, could not, replace his left ventricle, which had been too long deprived of oxygen during the initial cardiac mugging. His kidneys failed. He was dying, and off-the-shelf heart transplants don't often happen. His only choice—besides, his surgeon joked humourlessly, calling the funeral home and ordering a casket—was a heart assist device known as an LVAD, an internal pump to push blood through Oisín's blown-out left ventricle and out into the aorta and the rest of the body.

Oisín didn't know how exactly they began, the time loops that twisted Möbius-like through the surgical procedure and induced coma and months that followed, but he attributed the odyssey of his imagination to the suggestion of anesthesia. After sixty days, Oisín was discharged, his LVAD gear in a shoulder harness that looked like a suicide vest. He used a walker and moved slowly. Florence drove him home. Oisín looked out the window at the summer he'd lost, the fields along I-90 East going brown, the beans and corn. He wondered if his dogs Lloyd and Llama would remember him. He cried involuntarily, something that began the day he heard a children's choir moving along the hall in Mary Brigh singing songs. It reminded him of Africa. He missed Africa. He told himself, as soon as he was well enough, he would go back to Africa again, and he cried involuntarily, knowing he'd never go back to Africa, or a hundred other places he'd lived and worked and visited.

Over the winter, he led Lloyd and Llama along trails he'd once scampered and skied without ever once considering that he might never see the deep backwoods again. Sometimes, when he reached turnaround points, he stopped and sobbed for joy. He started writing poetry again for the first time in years. Snow, sleet, freezing rain, bitter wind and brutally cold temperatures did not daunt him. He hiked every day. Every day he wrote poetry, and more fiction. Every day he celebrated his achievements with beer or wine. Oisín, still not entirely convinced of life or death, was convinced, deeply, intellectually, that his life was a fiction—not untrue, as many naively believe fiction to be—a narrative, a story alive, a tale told and retold.

He rented a little office in a downtown storefront sort of kitty-corner from the Java Shoppe, which of course is where he met grown-up Lily Jo eleven years after he carried ten-year-old Joan from her mother's flooded kitchen. Oisín started an elite, coveted and poor-selling literary press, and twice a year published, *Spilt Milk*, an award-winning literary journal. He resigned from the EDA after seven years, and he and Florence sold their magnificent house, downsized, and transplanted again, this time to Winona, on the Mississippi River, home to two universities, a technical college, restaurants, movie theatres, a good job for Florence close to home, a literary culture Oisín fit comfortably into, an old brick storefront large enough to accommodate a small office and a large conference room for working with authors and hosting publishing and writing workshops.

So, it turned out that ten years after he failed heart transplant screening, fifteen years after his book "Oceans of Loam and Ice" was published and sold tepidly, and eight years after Lily Jo abruptly quit her job at the Java Shoppe to "find her place in the world," he noticed a patent leather black Tesla pull up in front of his office in old downtown Winona. A woman in a calf-length cashmere sweater, and a boy, maybe seven years old, got out and walked into Oisín's shop, cluttered with books by scores of authors he'd published, and copies of his magazine containing hundreds more writers.

The woman and the boy didn't acknowledge Oisín at first; they were drawn to the kiosks and book stands displaying Oisín's wares. Finally, she looked at him, still young to the old man, but strangely mature, making her appear both familiar and painfully beautiful in his eyes. "Did you write any of these?" she asked.

"One or two. But I publish a lot of literary authors and poets. Are you looking for anything in particular?" Oisín smiled at the boy. "I'm sorry but I don't publish children's books."

"Which ones are yours?" asked the wealthy woman. "I've already read "Oceans of Loam and Ice." I liked it very much."

"You actually read it?" Oisín replied, mildly shocked.

"I read some of the stories two or three times. I always knew you would be a good writer." She pushed out her hand to shake his. An elaborate water sprite surrounded by green leaves covered her wrist and the back of her hand. "You don't remember me, do you? I'm Joan. Lily Jo. You rescued me from the great flood all those years ago."

"Lily Jo?" Oisín, pulled on the strap of his heart-in-a-bag hanging on a hook screwed into the wall behind his desk so that he could only half stand. "I'll be darned. Lily Jo!" He wanted to unhook his bag to get up and hug her but just smiled, dumbfounded. "You know, when you worked at the Java Shoppe, I didn't recognize you from the flood, but I knew there was something familiar about you. I made the connection after you disappeared—left. You look like you're doing well.

94

That water sprite makes for a lovely tattoo, Lily Jo. Is it Ondine?"

"Yes, it is." Lily Jo smiled, confident, smothered in the artwork of her skin ink and colorful blouse under sweater; draped with jewelry: diamond bands and gold bracelets, pearls, and a simple medical alert pendant surrounded with rubies on a platinum chain around her long, sinewy neck. She traced Ondine with a manicured finger, her nails enameled in red. "She was a gift from me to myself. I am the river now."

"I can see that."

"Oisín, I got a new heart five years ago."

Oisín wrestled with the sudden urge to cry and won. "My God, that's fantastic," he said, dry-eyed. "And is this young lad your son?"

Lily Jo grinned. "This is Brendan."

"Brendan?"

"Yeah," she beamed. "My prince."

"Pleased to meet you, son. You must be proud of Ondine." Oisín took Lily Jo's hand in both of his and held it. "I think about you sometimes. I guess it's because of the way we met back in Bergen Creek flood."

"Like in your story 'Sea of Ice,' the woman on an island garden surrounded by nothing but water."

"You really have read Oceans," Oisín beamed, still fighting the urge to break down and bawl like a baby. "Would you like to sit? Brendan, can I get you a bottle of water? There's a saucer full of Kit Kats over there on the table."

The boy shook his head No, fixated by all the book covers.

Lily Jo took a chair. "I have to get going, but I've driven past here a hundred times and keep telling myself I need to stop and see you—"

"—about books."

"Yes, about books. I read a lot. You understand, I bet. When you spend weeks in the hospital, months in rehab, you have plenty of time to read."

"A new heart. Oh, I'm so happy for you."

"Thank you. How is your VAD?" Lily Jo glanced at the teardrop bag hooked to the wall.

Oisín had lived so long with his heart-in-a-bag that he often forgot about the precarious and onerous equipment; about how fragile he was with barely half a natural heart, dependent on dozens of pills daily; dependent on electricity, the heavy batteries in his bag during the day, a long extension cord connected to a transformer at night. He never quite slept well, never quite woke from looping dreams.

He drew a deep breath. "Still walking the back trails with my dog Lloyd, but he's getting old. Sabina died, oh boy, five years ago already. Dogs live such short lives. I think it's some kind of karmic punishment for being a human, the bond with a creature that dies and returns as another dog, and another dog, love and death." He stopped himself, grinned weakly and said, "Sorry. I ramble anymore when I talk, like I'm forever writing a first draft."

"Do you remember," Lily Jo asked in a very studious voice, "writing these lines?

What's light is dark, dark is light.
Hot is cold and what's cold is hot.
What's right is wrong, wrong is right.
What isn't is and what was is not."?

"They're from Oceans; that I know for certain. Help me. What was the story again?"

"'River of Ice,'" Lily Jo laughed, proud to have stumped the auteur. "It's the last story in the book; the one where spacetime is an infinitely wide Möbius Strip, which is a metaphor for the icy whirlpools; the woman in the story is born from the whirlpool; born fully grown with a spontaneous pregnancy somehow; and somehow, she spontaneously terminates it. In a heartbeat her mood swings from happy to sad. Time twists her life so that she's on the underside of where she was moments before, 'where what isn't is and what was is not.' She tries and tries but she can't have children which means she can't find love—the river of ice—but she has her garden; every beautiful rose and lily is a child, just as every word in your story embodies a lifeforce. The rivers rise and ice covers the land, except the island where her garden grows. She is the river and the garden just as she is her own mother and her own child. I love that story, because I feel I am she, that you have somehow created me again and again in flowing, swirling, upside-down words. Ideas and images."

Oisín couldn't take his eyes off Lily Jo when a dark wraith descended from the ceiling and slowly enclosed him in a shroud woven from time and imagination. "It's not too late for me to rewrite the ending, Lily Jo. Or the beginning. We can begin again. Delete the past and start over."

"Is that what you believe?" she asked, devoutly compliant. "I think this is the end."

"I don't want it to end," he replied, his eyes flushed with tears. "You are me as much as you are she. Don't go, Lily Jo. My dear child, words cannot describe how I am going to miss you if the book is finished. Where is your son? Where is my boy Brendan?"

"I don't have a son, Oisín. Brendan is our father and our mother; Brendan is you reborn and dead again. All streams flow into the sea, but the sea is not full."

Forever etched on the surface of the water far overhead, disconnected from time holding him down: a sack of vital organs overtaken by cantankerous tissue and blood vessels: the loop of time is fluid—Oisín nodded and said, "I'm not afraid of the flow of time, but I can't leave yet Lily Jo. Florence and the animals. My writing isn't ..."

The room grew darker and colder. Lily Jo squeezed Oisín's hand and rubbed the back of his shoulder. "I am not here, Ocean," she whispered. "You are not here." The warmth of her flesh flowing his. "I am blood."

"... ready. I'm not finished."

The writer Brendan Sullivan left his body at the exact moment he finished marking up the stories in his new collection, "Thermotropic Lotus," fiction he'd painstakingly crafted and revised over the first cold, dark winter he spent with a left-ventricular assist device perfusing his blood without pulse, floodwater pumped back into the river through a fire hose, irritating the walls of tiny blood vessels and arteries in the gastrointestinal tract—constant suffocation, end-stage heart failure, end-stage kidney failure, infection at the driveline site, blood clots massing inside the LVAD pump spinning at ten thousand two hundred RPMs.

Brendan's forty-year-old Rotring drafting pencil slipped through his fingers. He pushed himself up and out of his worn-out arts-and-crafts-style oak recliner to watch the scene unfold from a corner of the room, near the ceiling, in front of the cold air return above his chair—his physical body wobbling upon ankles, feet bent aside under his shins, useless.

When there was no more blood to pump, Mr. Sullivan's time loop snapped. He vanished into sensory emptiness for a heartbeat and reappeared, his body now ten feet from the foot of the recliner, the pages of his precious unfinished manuscript scattered around the den darkened by February gloom. He watched himself stumble drunkenly against a large flat-screen TV perched on a pedestal beside an oak bookshelf. Imploding downward into an old lap blanket, Brendan saw the flat-screen TV sprayed with hard-stitched spines and brittle dust jackets fall on top of him.

When finally he woke in his body again, eye level with his cat Poivre, his pajama bottoms and robe were soaked with piss. He lay twenty-five feet away from his chair in the kitchen hall near the back stairs. His LVAD batteries, controller, and wires spilled from his suicide vest, guts and data splayed open, vulnerable. The force of the fall had yanked off the critical driveline anchor glued to his abdomen at the site of the suppurating wound where the driveline cable pierced his flesh and snaked up inside to the pump plumbed onto his aorta.

The constant pressure of the LVAD caused an internal GI bleed, a gusher from a pinhole. Bleeding out. No blood pressure. No oxygen-rich hemoglobin. His intestines filled with blood.

Somehow, Brendan managed to crawl on his stomach within stretching distance of the cell phone lying beside the recliner where his sudden slow-motion death had begun. He dropped his head to the carpet and took a moment of looping reflection to consider the opportunity before him to put an end to the frustrating cycle of life and fiction, time and water, fulfillment and drowning, simply by lying there, the smell of wet dogs and a dying man releasing all of his fluids—"I have to sleep."

Suddenly Brendan felt Lloyd and Llama licking his feet. He wracked his eyes upward to see the opaque underside of the Möbius Strip roped with an icy river. The broken man closed his eyes in meditation and eased himself unafraid back into the rapids, then called 911.

7. OLD MAMADOU

Cowering under roofs of moldering grey thatch, the poorly constructed mud huts of Otou made the tiny village look like a colony of nut-brown termite mounds pounded flat by seasonal rains that twice annually visited le Plateau Batéké, a fifty-thousand-year-old deposit of windblown Kalahari sand. The appearance of destitution didn't matter to Otou's two hundred fifty hunters and farming women, nor to their runny nosed children, their fiery hunting dogs, scrawny black chickens and bleating goats.

Otou was home, and home was history, something to be talked about by ebony men enjoying cola nuts and daily fires in their exclusive *corps de gardes*, and by bare shouldered women huddled together on the dirt floor of a neighbor's cuisine smoking hand carved pipes filled with dried plants from the bountiful forest to dull the monotony of cleaning fish with only their fingers or slicing manioc leaves into blackened clay pots.

They talked about what they knew about: their home. Their home was history, family and place and time. The villagers talked for hours on end, every day, analyzing their history, embellishing it, lying about it, endlessly revising it.

Old Mamadou lived apart from the others, below Otou on the Boa Plain, gently arching hills of deep sand, termite spires and scrub brush as far as the eye could see. He constructed an uncommonly durable hut from hard, dark, mushroom shaped termite hearts dotting the arid landscape. "Vivant," is how the withered man proudly described his stack of meticulously hand carved bricks. Termite workers chattered incessantly, boring from block to block, in a sense weaving Mamadou's house into a single mass with their simple enzyme.

The inhabitants of Otou looked with disdain down upon Mamadou's homestead, his ancient termite house, always a handful of banana trees and coffee plants secure inside a meandering bramble fence. In their collective view, the old man was a *fou*, a crazy abomination whose proclivity for sorcery could not be tolerated. Mamadou was just a boy, nine years old, when Chef Ndaka Jean Louis drove him out of Otou for throwing a lightning bolt clear across the plateau to the village of Njangolou where it killed the Chef's only brother.

Even fifty years after the Chef's harsh ruling, Mamadou had no reason to doubt the villagers who threatened whenever they passed near his house that they would chop down a hardwood tree, cut a hole in the trunk and wedge his foot there permanently if he ever tried to use his reckless magic again.

Mamadou cooked for himself. He slept with no one but his phantoms. Over the course of the year, every year for five decades, the celibate old man survived alone by chopping down tall trees near the river then clearing his own plantation with fire to prepare for women's work. He cultivated manioc, *aubergines, ignames,* taro and amaranth. Afraid to hunt large game in the *bosquets*—small islands of forest dotting the white sea of plateau sand—for fear that hunters from Otou and surrounding villages might in turn hunt him, Mamadou concocted ingenious traps to ensnare, impale, decapitate or suffocate small birds, mammals and reptiles wandering through the sprawling tract that had belonged to his mother.

One day, Mamadou spotted French soldiers marching across the distant horizon in the direction of Otou. By wading along river shallows, the fast-moving water pure green like broken panes of thick glass, Mamadou was able to get a good view of the French troops, two-thirds of them Africans, sweating in their heavy cotton uniforms under the burden of machetes, rifles, chains and neck irons. He overheard them discussing their orders to forcibly relocate the entire village of Otou off the plateau and down into the *forêt* where a new laterite road built by the Portuguese sliced through rival Bapanou land.

Mamadou raced back to the termite house, grabbed two precious cartouches for his shotgun and struggled up the long hill through shin deep sand to warn the villagers of Otou.

Before Mamadou could reach the elders' smoky *corps de garde* surrounded by mud huts melting on rotting poles and wattle, a swarm of gangly schoolboys descended on him, disarmed him, bound his gnarled hands behind his back and wrestled him into a cool mango grove.

Old papas looked on approvingly. Women cackled. Children spat derision. Uninhibited village boys forced the old man's foot through a hole carved into a palm tree lying on its side over a wine tapping trench. They drove in a bamboo wedge so tightly that Mamadou's ankle shattered. Old Mamadou slumped back on the log babbling incoherently about shackles while the villagers returned to Otou, laughing the whole way, confident that Mamadou's lightning would not strike them.

8. Sirènes

O live, I want you to cut me!" The Political Officer assigned to the American Embassy in Kinshasa was so infatuated with the voluptuous Congolese girl, his normally baritone voice betrayed a squeak of latent boyishness.

A pragmatic *villageoise*, Olivia practically spit out her Diet Dr. Pepper. *"Quoi?"*

"Scar me. I want scars like the ones on your shoulders, only right here, under my eyes across both cheekbones. I'll get a knife."

Olivia wrapped herself in a dark turquoise Navajo blanket, her clear eyes eclipsed by disbelief and weariness while Dr. L.L. Langdon (PhD, anthropology, Georgetown 1979) scampered naked into the kitchen and returned with another beer, a clean towel, a sharpening stone and his wife's best butcher knife.

"Jean, non! Je ne peux pas!"

"Mais tu peut, Olive!" Dr. Langdon waved the knife recklessly under his eyes. (On a Fulbright grant to Zaire in 1977-78, he studied traditional warrior-sorcery.) *"Tssst! Tssst! Fini. C'est tout."*

"Jean, non."

Ignoring her objection, he shouted, *"Attendez!"* The senior diplomat's mind rapidly seized on details of the ritual he was about to perform as he darted back into the pantry. Inside an upright freezer, behind a stack of frozen burritos from the commissary, he removed a plastic panel concealing Anasazi Chief Tuba Cecil's snake bone necklace, the remains of David Livingstone's desiccated heart, a one hundred year old agreement between Daka Bwana and King Leopold II of Belgium establishing the utopian colony of Sena Tatu, and an extraordinarily heavy fleck of priceless Ekwateurium he had removed from the freezing brass testicles of the Manneken Pis in Brussels on the cusp of the New Year. Dr. Langdon grabbed the family Bible from a shelf in the dining room, stopped to program Bach's Toccata and Fugue in D Minor to play over and over and over, then plopped down cross legged under the halo of stormy candlelight to face the sweet, uneducated village woman Olivia. Stinking of cold sex, he spread out between them all the contraband he'd foraged since arriving in Zaire eighteen months earlier. They were computer game sorcerers whose only mission was to figure out the special artifacts and use them without destroying their fantasy world in the process.

Guided by invisible forces, the crazed diplomat lit-up another marijuana cigarette, inhaling the sublime drug deeply and washing it down with a long swig of ice-cold Tembo before prying open the gold box containing a moldy truffle, the last remains of the blackened heart of a Scottish Missionary whose eviscerated corpse was carried across Africa and shipped to England for burial in 1873. Next, Dr. Langdon rolled the ponderous Ekwa Stone carefully across the brittle lease to Sena Tatu until the radiant speck rested upon Daka Bwana's effusive signature. Covering the dark-shimmering Ekwateurium with his right hand, careful not to burn his palm as he had burned his leg with it in Brussels, he solemnly draped the Anasazi shaman's necklace of Arizona snake bones around Olivia's neck, wrapped her tiny fingers around the walnut hilt of the carving knife and guided its whetted blade to his pale face, reading from Judges 21:21 to keep from screaming as she slashed him.

"'And see, and behold, if the daughters of Shiloh come out to dance in dances, then come ye out of the vineyards, and catch you every man his wife of the Sirènes of Shiloh.'"

"C'est quoi ça?" Olivia asked, clearly excited by Dr. Langdon's blood dripping off her elbows. *"C'est une formule magique?"*

"Oui, Olive, une formule magique."

⚹

Just before sunrise, when Dr. Langdon had tried to sneak Olivia out of the house before the day shift of Embassy security guards arrived, Papa Nganza, an old, loyal night sentinel, studied his American boss with a horrified expression, reserving his most contemptuous gaze however for Olivia. To defuse a potentially ugly domestic melee, Dr. Langdon sent the old man scrambling down the street two blocks to the Intercon to fetch a taxi. Nganza quickly arrived back at the house and planted himself defiantly beside the haggard American seconds before a dented, lime green Mercedes chugged lazily out of the darkness into the inky cartoon of Dr. Langdon's driveway. Olivia threw herself like a sack of potatoes into the backseat. She waved sleepily and promised to return after dark for dinner as agreed.

"I'll bring banana leaves for your wounds," she mumbled sickly and smiled. "That's all I can do. You should see a doctor, Jean." Dr. Langdon had told her his name was Jean Rowlands after she told him she wanted to be his secretary. Dr. Langdon chose the name Rowlands as a fitting sobriquet for his altering-self. The Welsh explorer, Henry Morton Stanley, born in 1841, was originally christened John Rowlands by his parents who would soon send him to a Dickensian workhouse for destitute boys.

Olivia's remarks in French provoked a Lingala tirade from Papa Nganza. It was clear from the anger burning in Olivia's reddened, sleep-deprived eyes that the old man was chewing her out for screwing a mundele while the wife was away in Europe, and, as if that wasn't bad enough, for carving her secret sign into the stupid mundele's ashen face.

Dr. Langdon tried to mediate. *"Papa Nganza, s'il vous plait, Papa !"*

The old sentinel refused to listen. Dr. Langdon finally had to spin the trusted sentinel around physically, walk him back to the guard shack and wave for the taxi man to leave before he would shut up.

"Au revoir, Jean," Olivia called as the taxi backed into the darkness. Dr. Langdon wasn't sure if three-quarters of a million zaires to buy a sack of manioc for her sister's family and some clothes, shoes, cosmetics for herself would bring Olivia back or get rid of her for good, nor could he decide which would be the better outcome.

Nganza admonished, "No banana leaves on those scars, not yet, patron. I will go to the market and bring you village medicine." The old man cocked the worn visor of the Embassy guard cap back on his head of salty hair, allowing porch light to shine across dark scars carved into both of his temples. They looked like claw marks, five black slashes on either side of his mahogany brow. "I'll go now, patron," he said with a mix of reverence and deference.

"Très bien, Papa, merci beaucoup."

"Wash the scars with whiskey," advised the old patriarch, a man with two wives, fourteen children, nine of them males.

"I already did that."

"Do it again." Papa Nganza hesitated before leaving.

"Is there something else? Do you need money? Let me get some."

"No, patron, you can pay me when I get back from the market."

"Then what is it?"

Papa Nganza sternly regarded Dr. Langdon, twenty-five years his junior. He whispered, *"Le SIDA ..."*

The white-haired Embassy guard might as well have hit the career diplomat in the head with a club. Dr. Langdon's breath turned icy cold, but he did his best to remain composed. "SIDA?" he asked as if he did not know what le SIDA was.

Curling his small fingers into a fist and slapping the top of it with his other palm, Papa Nganza arched his eyebrows quizzically. *"Ça va, patron?"*

Dr. Langdon grinned like an idiot though his blood had changed into gasoline. *"Ça va, Papa."*

Papa Nganza smiled for the first time. He was evidently satisfied that AIDS would not be a problem for a man who had screwed all night without a condom then forced a strange prostitute to draw his blood from two huge facial wounds using a thirteen-inch carving knife. Back in the house, numb, dead tired, Dr. Langdon grabbed another beer and flopped down on the front room carpet. Thankful only that it was Saturday, he lay there in a state of absolute terror and shame, staring up at the ceiling fan, still extraordinarily aroused.

ɛ

A slow-motion dawn painted dark pastels in ventilator blocks spaced along the wall just below the high ceiling of Dr. Langdon's comfortable villa. His mind, quiet throughout the nightlong spree with Olivia, had switched to cognitive high alert. A hundred different voices shouting at once disparaged the only friend he knew, the one who had deserted him at the nadir of the full moon for a destitute *putain*. Haunted by a thundering refrain, "Fear and loathing, fear and loathing, fear and loathing ..." he propped himself up on one elbow to drain the remaining three fingers from a fifth of Johnny Walker into the least bloody of several bloody towels. Truly understanding Gonzo's words for the first time, the middle-aged diplomat draped the towel over his face and inhaled desperately. "Fear and fucking loathing."

Multiple orgasms, among the host of carnal pleasures he had experienced with the young African woman, pushed fear and loathing together with all things familiar and alien. Opposites mixed in his blood, integrity with depravity, brilliance with stupidity, life with death. He pulled the towel down off his forehead and opened his swollen eyes. He felt the whirling blades of the ceiling fan fall into his face and chew his usually youthful, cheerful features to a pulp. He passed out, sadly convinced that he would soon die.

Awakened around 8 a.m. by the sound of a night sentinel's temperate voice calling from the front porch, Dr. Langdon crawled to the screen door clutching a wad of newly printed ten thousand Z-notes he had bought from the same black-market money changer who sold him an Okapi cigarette pack stuffed with neatly rolled marijuana joints. Old, white-haired Papa Nganza knelt on the red tile porch to dress his patron's wounds with bright yellow paste then covered the paste with scarlet powder and the bitter flesh of a jungle succulent, carefully cinching the poultice over the mortified diplomat's ears with a supple broadleaf. Fighting back guilty tears, Dr. Langdon looked into the gentle old man's face. He saw his pitiful life, a black stone eroded smooth except for bone deep, brightly burning lacerations ringing where his future should have been.

&

A few months earlier, Dr. Langdon and his wife, Rebecca Lewis, the respected theoretical physicist and daughter of the recent Nobel Prize winner in economics, mathematician Hanson Lewis, were in Amsterdam for New Year's. They argued on every street corner after leaving the Van Gogh Gallery, ostensibly because of a dispute over Vincent's portrait of the Postman Roulin. Their mutual anger escalated until Rebecca suddenly ducked into the KLM office and purchased two seats on a hop to Frankfurt leaving in three hours, one for herself and one for Bottom, the embattled Langdon-Lewis's six-year-old daughter.

Dr. Langdon defiantly refused to consider spending New Year's with scientists from the Heavy Ion Lab in Darmstadt, Germany. So, the family checked out of the hotel and Rebecca hailed a cab.

"Who is it you plan to spend New Year's Eve with then, Beck, Jon Beaumont?" Dr. Langdon grasped at straws.

"Oh Christ, Lang! What in the world is wrong with you?" Rebecca hissed. "Jon is a colleague and a friend! Listen, just like you with the investigation of Dag Hammarskjöld's death, I can't choose my colleagues. What's her name, the blonde woman from the Van Gogh Museum you've been sending all those documents to, the Swedish Ambassador's wife?"

"Widow. The Swedish Ambassador has been dead for almost five-years, Beck. And her name is Siv Colburg."

"Widow. Well, is Siv Colburg, the widow, the reason you're interested in a thirty-year-old plane crash?"

"Don't be ridiculous!"

"Don't you be ridiculous, Lang! I too am working on a question of great importance. Only I can't work in the modern world and live in Zaire at the same time unless I want to study AIDS or poverty, and that's not my calling. And I won't apologize for that! My work is physics. I am obsessed with it just as you are obsessed with your projects. That's why I can still give you the benefit of the doubt, Lang. We're both driven by our working minds, either that or we're both crazy. In any case, we don't have time to waste arguing about it in Amsterdam."

"Then don't go, Beck. I want to try, I really do. Why don't you come back to Zaire for two weeks? See how you feel? I want to hold you, massage your temples with your chin against my eyes. Beck, please."

"No!" She kissed her husband gently on the mouth, her salty tears dripping onto his upper lip. "Give Bottom a hug before we miss our flight," she groused.

Bottom stood a few feet away studying the slushy sidewalk, ignoring Mom and Dad. Dr. Langdon picked up his lovely daughter, hugged her, kissed her. "You can come and stay in Mommy's apartment, Daddy, until you get better. We have room, and we love you, don't we Mommy?" He loved the sound of her voice.

"Yes, we do, Bot, we love your Daddy." Rebecca sounded tired. She didn't look back as the cab sped away.

&

Dr. Langdon's swollen eyes cracked open. Dream escaped like a boat into fog. He caught one or two ceiling fan blades in mid-flight before they were erased in blur. Lying directly beneath the fan even, he could feel the oppressive noon heat of Kinshasa. Sick, dirty, deathly afraid to take the next step into his suddenly uncertain future, the career Foreign Service Officer stumbled upstairs past his daughter's deserted room into his deserted bedroom. Rebecca had been gone for months but half of her clothes still hung in the closet. On the dresser, there was a picture taken by a Lake Geneva ferry operator a decade earlier, the powerful Swiss waterspout blasting skyward behind Drs. Langdon and Lewis. Two carved boxes filled with Beck's jewelry sat on the vanity among her neatly arranged cosmetics, perfumes, combs, barrettes. They were a woman's things, dried flowers, a blue votive candle, aromatic sandalwood beads, little things that had meant precious little to Dr. Langdon until that very moment.

He undressed like a condemned man preparing for his last shower, a final private reflection back on his last request for a pleasure orgy before execution. Dr. Langdon stood under the hot spray, careful not to wash away Nganza's medication, preoccupied by the cacophony of voices tearing him apart inside, absolving him, scorning him, excusing him, cursing him. He imagined collapsing at supper with Olivia, his body covered with open sores. Alone he died only to be reborn as an adult, an explorer, a prophet. He wandered into the darkness and married a serpent. And he carved open the breast of Africa. And he reached inside. And he pulled out its beating heart. Then he dreamed he was only dreaming. The solace he desired disappeared when the shower ran caustic, cold, splitting his head open, clogging the drain with green slime.

ε

One of the oddest footnotes to the liberation of Kuwait in January 1991 was the fact that the corrupt dictatorship of Mobutu Sese Seko had rotated to a temporary seat on the Security Council, putting Zaire's Ambassador to the U.N. in the position of casting a critical vote in favor of authorizing the use of force against Saddam Hussein's corrupt dictatorship. Dr. Langdon rarely found an opportunity to discuss the future of the Persian Gulf, at least officially, because he was preoccupied with introducing his counterparts to the terms of the 1991 Foreign Assistance Act.

Terse and unambiguous when it came to Zaire, Congress had taken the unprecedented step of eliminating economic aid to Mobutu's regime, doubtless in response to the May 1990 massacre of as many as one hundred politically active students at the University of Lubumbashi. Despite Zaire's absurd but crucial role in punishing Iraq, Mobutu's government received no thanks more substantive from Washington than the well-liked Dr. Langdon's watered-down diplomacy. America, the undisputed winner of the Cold War, no longer felt constrained to appease flagrant offences committed by thieving despots like Mobutu Sese Seko.

It was about this time, early-1991, that Zairian doctors and nurses went on strike to protest low wages, rendering already scarce health services completely unreliable. The University closed. The entire civil service remained on permanent strike along with most government run parastatals companies. Transportation failed. The formal systems of budget and economy essentially ceased to function. Spiraling inflation and social entropy ravaged the poor. Most worrisome, at least from Dr. Langdon's informed point-of-view, were the signs of growing rancor within Mobutu's notoriously disloyal military.

"Lang-old-chum, get real, will you?" snickered Bollington Meade, the Deputy Chief of Mission who rigorously positioned himself between the Ambassador and his popular protégé, Dr. Langdon. Ambassador Strait, the Defense Attaché Colonel Blackburn, the CIA Special Assignment Officer Geraldo Silva, the Regional Security Officer Eagle-Two, the DCM and Dr. Langdon discussed Mobutu's recent decision to postpone long-promised Presidential elections.

"Boll, Zaire's military could turn against the civilian population in a heartbeat," Dr. Langdon snapped. "The merchants will be pillaged, the cities will be sacked, just to get even for too many months without pay."

"The Army is a joke!" Bollington scoffed. "They'd have to bring in French and Moroccan troops to pull it off, like they did in 78, and that's not bloody likely. You should know how it works by now. Good God, man, use your noggin!"

Geraldo Silva bummed a stick of Double Mint from Colonel Blackburn and wadded it into a lazy curl against his milky tongue. "We can't decide whose side we want to be on anymore, Mr. Ambassador. My motto's always been, pick a side to be on, be on that side, and pick on the other side," SA/JAO opined.

"This is a nation of minorities, Mr. Ambassador, close to five hundred of them, ethnic minorities, not coalitions, and now you must factor in one hundred fifty political parties. Elections will have to work like rounds in a basketball tournament, you know, where you have to lose twice before you're out. All those who make it to the finals automatically become ranking parliamentarians. Zaire needs a proportional representation system."

"Hogwash!" the DCM sputtered.

"Boll, without a series of primary elections to thin out the pack, without a transparent nomination process, fair campaigns, supervised polls, an honest vote count and some kind of proportional power sharing arrangement, you're going to have mayhem in a hundred different venues come election day!"

"Oh, give me a break, Dr. Langdon. The world is watching. If Zaire holds a vote tomorrow, we'll damn-well throw our support behind the winner."

"What support is that? Air strikes, Boll?"

"Lang, calm down," the Ambassador winked authoritatively. "Let Bollington make his point."

The DCM gloated, "We lay down the law. You think Zaire is going to try anything funny? Not likely, not after a perfect New World Order object lesson in Iraq."

"A perfect neo-colonial object lesson in hegemony, don't you mean, Boll? Le Guide is smarter than you think. Even if Mobutu's bogus National Conference produces an election timetable, Presidential candidates will still come straight out of the President's circle. The only way to beat Mobutu after twenty-five-years of entrenchment—if you're really serious— is to pop up out of the manholes firing, take over. Maybe we could get the World Bank to load the cabinet with expat advisors like we did in Liberia. That was a big success."

"Your problem isn't democracy," Bollington sputtered to find a rejoinder, "it's racism!"

"Racism? I am not a racist, Boll! I'm a realist. I suggest we convene a donor meeting to pledge funds to strengthen democratic institutions. Let the National Conference take place. I mean, if you just stop and think about it, Boll, the only hope for Zaire until a viable candidate emerges is Mobutu himself."

Everyone around the table except the Ambassador laughed out loud. "You're supporting Mobutu now?" Bollington scoffed.

The Ambassador cast a stern glance around the table. "Any other comments?" Evander Strait looked at his knuckles for a long time. "I think we're through for today. No doubt we'll have reason to revisit this subject. Thank you, gentlemen."

&

At the Van Gogh Museum in Amsterdam just after Christmas, Bottom, Dr. Langdon's only child, seemed mesmerized by the bold flowers, explosive stars, oaken peasants, green-faced women and troubled skies. The walls were filled with his fruit, his fish, his friends. Rebecca Lewis, whose mother Colette was born in Arles four-decades after Van Gogh left the south of France and returned to Paris, stopped frowning when she came to the painting of the Arles Drawbridge and a series of Rhone River landscapes. Dr. Langdon wandered on holding Bottom's tiny hand, his attention drawn to one picture in particular, the Arles Postman named Roulin.

"Who is that?" Bottom asked, her eyes sparking like the transparent eyes of the man in the painting.

"That's your great-great-great-grandpa."

"Lang! What are you telling her?" My glowering wife, hissing stunned and hurt, had crept up behind me.

"I'm speaking metaphorically about fatherhood, Beck. Is that all right with you?" Beck threw back her head arrogantly and spun around three hundred sixty degrees on her heel. "Popo had a great big reddish beard," the diplomat continued, "just like the Postman Roulin in Van Gogh's painting. When I was a boy, I used to sit on my father's lap and he would pull the beard around my face, disguising me with it, rubbing the smell of pipe tobacco and coffee all over me."

Rebecca exploded. "My God, what are you doing? Bottom understands that you grew up in an orphanage, baby."

"I'm not a baby!" Dr. Langdon snapped, startling a few gallery patrons who quickly moved along.

"Lang, please don't get started. Let's go somewhere else."

Bottom looked up, her eyes marbled like melting chocolate, and asked, "Is grandpa in the cemetery?"

Beck almost flipped. "Jesus! I cannot deal with this right now. Come on, Bottom, let's go get something to eat. Daddy, are you coming or not?"

Dr. Langdon studied the Postman who once carried Van Gogh's desperately insightful letters. Roulin wore a poorly fitted blue coat with pale yellow piping, a blue postman's hat plopped on his head like a dollop of pudding. He had a dizzying, swirling red beard and judgmental, wallpaper eyes that floated unevenly, painted flowers raining down from the light green background.

"I'll be along, just give me five more minutes with the old man."

"Lang, don't do this to yourself, don't do it to us. Put your mind to making this vacation work and it will, I promise you, babe."

Rebecca's angry husband whipped around ready to argue but could not summon the strength. "Bottom, why don't you go with Mom and get us a table at the Red Windmill. Order me the grilled Capitaine and a Heineken, Beck, will you please?"

"Don't be sad, Daddy," Bottom sighed.

"I'm not sad, sweetie. You go with your mom now."

Dejected, Dr. Langdon turned back to Roulin. The entire bottom quarter of the canvas formed a massive rectangle of paint conjuring up Roulin's rumpled, double-breasted uniform. His giant outer lapel looked like a slab of modeling clay. Three oversized hexagonal buttons marked the vertices of a dominant triangle cleaving his beard into two great horse heads whose ears were woven through the postman's wavy moustache and up into his sideburns. Van Gogh had that special ability to imbue many, many details with the singular quality of being the most important to the composition. That was his insanity at work, no hierarchy, everything equally critical, everything critically critical. Dr. Langdon's eyes began and ended at Roulin's hat, a puddle of blue with the word *Postes* embroidered between narrow yellow bands. Yellow and blue flowers floated around Roulin's head and shoulders surreally as if someone had reached into the canvas from above and sprinkled them.

"Excuse me, sir, can you tell me, why does the Postman have such a thick beard when his son's is so thin?"

Dr. Langdon's head jerked against the brutality of the interruption, finding, when he turned, a woman of such mature beauty that only her dark-blue business suit mercifully suppressed an otherwise blinding aura. He cleared his throat. Words slipped out mechanically. "The Postman must be twenty-years-older than his son," he replied, "at least."

The blond smiled. "I don't think they look like father and son at all. Do you?"

The couple strolled together past more haunted landscapes, stopping nonchalantly at the portrait of a man with a boy's face, a boy's thin moustache and flushed cheeks drawn upon a darkish, dingy green background. His raven hair, mostly hidden beneath a floppy black fedora two sizes too big, languished grey at the temples. A sharp, striking widow's peak creased his brow like an axe blade, punctuating the image of worry sketched in wrinkles and weakness. Sad, watery eyes, pouting mouth, the most melancholy face Dr. Langdon had ever seen, belonged to Armand Roulin, the Postman's son.

"You're right, if I didn't know better, I'd say Armand was not Roulin's son."

The blonde's smile revealed satisfaction. "Would you like to join me for a cigarette in the atrium, Dr. Langdon?" she asked. "I just purchased a fresh package of Drum."

Momentarily disoriented, the diplomat scrambled to remember who was the woman in the tailored suit carrying a matching cashmere coat and scarf in the strap of a leather briefcase slung confidently over her shoulder. His mind flashed still photos of a meeting he had attended in the office of the Under Secretary of State for Africa, Thurmond Whittaker, just before leaving for Zaire. Also attending was Siv Colburg, the youthful widow of Bo Colburg, the Swedish Ambassador to the US who died suddenly in 1987 at the age of seventy-two.

"Siv, I wasn't sure if you would remember our year-old agreement to rendezvous here today."

The Swedish Ambassador's widow extended an alabaster hand. Not the chalky sculpture they appeared, her fingers were warm and moist and soft. "My draft report on the thirtieth anniversary review of the facts surrounding Dag Hammarskjöld's death is due in Stockholm on the fifth of January." Her perfect British accent sounded as if every syllable had been carefully turned on a lathe.

"Shall we have that cigarette, Dr. Langdon?"

Dr. Langdon stared deep into her eyes darkened dramatically by the color of her expensive blue jacket. His wife's almond-colored eyes matched the reflection of Siv's understated silk blouse reflected in tiny windows etched upon her irises. The desire to talk to Siv throbbed painfully like a phantom limb. They sat among hanging plants under spacious skylights ladling the winter sun into the Van Gogh's white walled galleries.

&

Dr. Langdon continued working long past staff meeting. With Beck and Bottom living in Germany, he often stayed late at the Embassy. Around twenty-two hundred hours he signed out at the Marine Guard station and drove slowly through

Kinshasa's deserted streets, aimlessly, anonymously. He felt especially shitty, like he'd been crushed by a meteor made of sorrow. A moon full of sorrow floated high above the dirty blue city. He selected a cassette tape containing a litany of nocturnes by Debussy and rolled down a narrow street with his lights off, the way *Kinois* taxi drivers did, the London Orchestra drifting in and out of view as musical fog slowly enveloped the night.

"Nuages." Dr. Langdon pronounced the sensuous French title, referring to himself in the second person. "Good choice, Armand old boy."

After an aimless drive along the Zaire River cataracts below Ilebo Pool, Dr. Langdon fished his blue Peugeot through sand clogging the traffic circle at Seven-Corners and rolled lazily back into town on *Trente Juin*. His eyes adjusted to the eerie, orangish glow of halogen streetlamps recently provided by the Japanese Government. Gray clouds spread across the black sky like spilt milk glazing the dirty moon. Street cats combed themselves with their tongues alongside the road, purring prostitutes preening in the half-light, hissing. All the way from *Kintambo* to the leaning minaret of the new mosque across from Hamburger House, whores crept from the darkness of the tree-lined street, silverfish a dank basement, to show off their goods for passing headlights. He flicked the Peugeot's on.

"Tssss! Tssss!" they called in the macabre tradition of the Zaire's women of the night, showing off their legs, their asses, their breasts, twirling in the street to display the costumes of sex. One whore pulled her sequined top down, proudly urging a pair of brown, ebony-nippled breasts to spring free. "Tssss! Tssss!"

Craving scotch and ice and midnight, Dr. Langdon raced impulsively into the heart of the city. His mind a dull needle, he screamed wildly through the well-to-do Gombe district without stopping until he pulled into an angled parking space in front of a small restaurant called Sur le Pouce. He locked the car, handed a crippled beggar five thousand zaires to watch the sidewalk, and slipped unsteadily, mindlessly next door into the Piano Bar.

A small jazz band serenaded well-dressed expats and perfumed Africans packing the tiny cabaret. The nameless diplomat hurriedly downed two double shots of Johnny Walker and an icy Castel at the bar where the unmistakable electricity of a woman close by made his hair stand on end. He smelled her soap and eventually turned his head. An attractive young woman bathed in colored lights smiled at him, her arms folded under her breasts, a baggy T-shirt tucked into the waist of her short skirt revealing a desirably youthful figure.

"Bon soir, monsieur," she flirted.

Dr. Langdon replied, *"Bon soir,"* and neurotically turned back to his drink.

"Coka pour moi?" she demanded bluntly.

Dr. Langdon dumped five dollars' worth of grimy zaires on the bar, enough for a glass of Coke. The woman did not say thank you, but Dr. Langdon felt free to study her while she chewed the expensive ice. She was very black, pure and colorless as coal, her face smooth like a cold pond, her expression betraying no roughness, her lucid eyes asking no questions, nor her moist lips, full and red, nor her silent pink tongue juggling broken ice around behind her perfectly white teeth.

After a couple more scotches, Dr. Langdon paid up. His mind was profoundly, conspiratorially silent as he turned toward the door and squeezed past the girl to go. She pushed herself against him, cradling his arm deep in the cleavage of her breasts, the back of his hand flat against her warm belly.

"Je vais aller avec vous." she asked him, she told him.

Without debate about volition, conditions, consequences, the diplomat nodded quickly and pushed through the crowd to the door. He unlocked his car and climbed in. He could have sped away, but he did not. He unlocked the passenger door and the girl slipped inside gracefully. He pushed the tape back into the player and drove in silence except for Debussy's nocturnal *Sirènes* who beckoned the darkness to wring out poetry like a mangle crushing dirty water from half-clean sheets. A sea of black, black night engulfed his ship. He dragged brittle chains down empty streets paved with bone light.

"J'adore la musique classique," she said.

"Oui?" he responded. Nothing worked in his head.

"Are we going to a hotel, monsieur?"

"No, no. I'm just driving. Where are you going?"

"Moi?"

"Do you live around here? I'll drop you somewhere."

"Moi?" She laughed. Dr. Langdon got his first glimpse of her face without the veil of bar lighting. She was younger than he first thought, and painfully pretty, wearing no make-up other than the bright red wound ringing her sensuous mouth. She sat on her hands, leaning forward, unrelaxed, pointing at a darkened building with her lips as the Peugeot shambled down the dark street. *"L'Ambassade Portugais?"* she asked.

"Oui."

"Are you Portuguese, monsieur?"

"Moi?" The Political Officer had to laugh. "Non."

"Allemande?"

"I'm not German. I'm an American."

"Oh. I like Americans. I know a clean hotel where we can go. It's not far."

"We're not going to a hotel."

"We're not? But, monsieur, I need the money. Let's go to a hotel. I'll do anything you want. One hundred thousand."

"One hundred thousand?"

"Seventy thousand. My body is nice, you'll like it, I have big papayas."

"How old are you?"

"Eighteen."

"Eighteen?"

"Seventeen."

"Do you go to school? Why aren't you at home?"

"I want to be a secretary. Do you need a secretary?"

"You studied to be a secretary?"

"No. But I finished elementary school. You can teach me to be your secretary."

"I don't need a secretary."

"What is your name?"

"My name? Rowlands, Jean."

Olivia crooned, "Jean ..."

&

Siv Colburg smiled and ignited another hand-rolled cigarette with her petite gold lighter. "Dr. Langdon, do you remember, as we rode down the State Department elevator from the Seventh Floor, you told me that your interest in Dag Hammarskjöld went much deeper than archives and classified memoranda? You said your earliest memory of the Congo was of hearing about Patrice Lumumba and Mr. Hammarskjöld on television. You must have been a very sensitive child."

Dr. Langdon's mouth twitched with unpronounceable words. He managed to wave his hand in the direction of the portrait of Armand Roulin. "Both my father and my wife's mother shared a passion for Van Gogh. My father looked something like the Postman Roulin and my wife's mother, who looked nothing like Roulin, was born in Arles."

"Arles, really?"

"Do you know who Armand Roulin is?" he stammered passionately.

"You mean the real person in the painting you insisted that I incorporate into a password in the event that one of us had uncovered proof of conspiracy to assassinate Dag Hammarskjöld? I must confess," she laughed seductively, "I came to Amsterdam as much to see if I could deliver my espionage lines as to find out what you had learned. But to answer your question, Doctor, no, who is the postman's son?"

Instinctively, Dr. Langdon smothered Siv's hand in his and began to gently caress her fingertips. "Armand was one of only a few friends Vincent Van Gogh had when he lived in Arles. Just before Christmas in 1888, fed up with Paul Gauguin's domineering manner, Van Gogh, in a delusional rage, tried to hack off his own ear. There was little a drunken loser like Armand Roulin could do to mitigate the poor artist's dementia or ease his horrible, self-inflicted suffering. Armand had too many problems of his own."

Siv Colburg gave Dr. Langdon a strange look, doting, lonely. "He did?" she asked.

"Oh yes, many. Armand's father, the blue postman, was tyrannical and chronically disappointed with his son. Van Gogh painted Armand, dejected and hung over like you see him in the portrait, in November 1888. On December twenty-third of that same year, Van Gogh mutilated his ear. In January, he painted the infamous self-portrait with the bandage covering the right side of his head. And in February and March 1889, with the promise of spring again changing the quality of the light, he painted the Postman Roulin. Sergeant Pepper."

Siv squeezed Dr. Langdon's thumb. "As any Swede will tell you, winter can be very depressing. Christmas only makes it worse. Spring is life, dear man."

Dr. Langdon wanted to take her mouth in his own, her knees and toes, but patted her hand instead. "I have to go. My wife has been waiting."

The Swedish Ambassador's widow fumbled awkwardly with her things. She shoved the pouch of Drum into her purse, gathered up her coat and scarf. "You'll contact me then, before I submit my final report in May?"

"I will, I promise." Siv extended her hand with a memorable smile, leaning forward to peck Dr. Langdon's cheeks with three kisses. Their noses brushed as she pulled away; he felt her breath on his tongue.

"Good," she said. "You have my card. Send any additional information you come across to my office."

"I'll try to think of something clever to lure you back here again," he laughed nervously. "Well, goodbye. I've enjoyed seeing you, Siv."

"Likewise, Dr. Langdon."

&

By Monday morning, most of the swelling around Dr. Langdon's eyes had disappeared leaving only blue bruises and bloody, centimeter wide slashes over both cheekbones. He put Olivia into a taxi at six a.m. and sent her to the Zaire-American Clinic for a routine physical and a battery of blood tests required of all prospective domestiques before they could be cleared to work in the homes of official Americans. Then he dressed his wounds himself, fighting dizziness and nausea as he applied Papa Nganza's paste, powder and plants, and covered his gashes with clean, white gauze and tape. Looking like he'd been shot twice in the face, he hurried into work early to beat the influx of diplomats.

Corporal Russ Black stood guard behind the Marine hardline. He buzzed the door lock, took a second look at the U.S. Embassy Third Secretary's battered face and turned white. "Dr. Langdon, what happened, did you have an accident, sir?"

Until that moment, the seasoned diplomat had not yet chosen a lie from among the millions of excuses for his appearance cluttering every conscious thought since early Saturday morning. Resisting the desire to shake Corporal Black's hand for forcing him to choose an alternative reality, he eyed the young, good looking Marine solemnly. "Friday night, driving in from Seven Corners? One of those huge transport trucks, no lights on."

"I hate it when they do that, sir. Think they're saving gas."

"Right. Well, he ran me off Justice and I went into the sewer. Somebody had stolen the covers."

"Those bastards! Are you ok?"

"I hit the steering wheel, as you probably guessed, cut up my cheekbones pretty good."

"Lucky you didn't break your nose."

124

"No, you can say that again."

"What about your vehicle, sir?"

"That's the irony. All the car needs is alignment, otherwise she's fine. A Belgian in a Pajero pulled me out. I'll be ok."

The first thing Dr. Langdon did when he got to his office was place a couple of calls to his wife in Germany. Rebecca wasn't at her apartment or the lab, so he left a message on her machine.

"Beck, it's me. Miss you. Miss Bot. Give her my love. Haven't gotten any mail for a while now. I just wanted to say I was thinking about you. No need to call back if you're busy. Love you both. Bye now."

In the forty-eight hours since his little peccadillo with Olivia, Dr. Langdon had learned to anticipate the attack of angry inner voices a second or less before he lapsed into involuntary self-examination. As he cradled the phone, the noise started again, the poison voices, the cries of helplessness, the tedious psychosis, the self-inflicted, heart-felt paralysis of metastasizing guilt. He didn't have to look up, he just knew that the Ambassador stood in the doorway, Bollington Meade chafing over his boss's shoulder to catch a glimpse.

"Lang?" the Ambassador interrupted. "The Marine guard said you ... oh my God! Dr. Langdon, what happened to you?"

Dr. Langdon looked the Ambassador in the eye, shook his head and repeated the lie he had fabricated for the Marine Guard. "It was an accident, sir. Went into a drain ditch. Knew no sirens would come save me, so when a Belgian offered to pull me out of the mess I was in, well, sir, I took him up on it."

9. Regime of Bananas

erman Schmidt, a civil engineer from Kalona, Iowa, set out alone to cross le Plateau Batéké in eastern Gabon carrying three cases of canned sardines, five boxes of Laughing Cow cheese and a flour sack crammed with oven fresh French bread he planned to share with villagers when he arrived at his destination. Herman's lifeline to-and-from the Plateau, a hard-working Toyota HJ-47, stooped under the weight of supplies on that maiden voyage to Ali-Ga. Ali-Ga, population two hundred when school was out.

The French engineering firm SOLOGAB posted Herman Schmidt in Ali-Ga for the twelve to eighteen months it would take him to survey three new bridge sites and twenty-five kilometers of stabilized roadway the oil rich government of Gabon planned to build. When completed, the Plateau highway linking sparsely populated villages scattered along the Gabon-Congo border from Akeni to Lekoni would bring changes far more monumental as any concrete bridge.

Besides his laser theodolite, portable computer and drawing table, Herman carried an old Fender acoustic six string he'd picked up for a hundred bucks in a Washington D.C. pawnshop, a ballistic quality canvas duffel bag bulging with khaki shorts, comfortable footwear, T-shirts and American toothpaste, his reference books, his sketch books, a dozen paperback political thrillers and his journal, a black book of blank pages.

A surplus French Foreign Legion headquarter tent Herman lugged clean across the country from Libreville would serve as both home and office until he could build himself a small house. Seven full *cassiers* of Régab beer minus three road bottles chattered like a classroom of practical jokers over every washboard bump.

Essential mechanic's and carpenter's tools added considerable weight in the back, as did several long Okoumé planks to make himself a nice bed and a three-inch thick, feather weight slab of polyurethane foam that would serve as his mattress. The two-hundred-liter barrel of diesel fuel tied down behind the driver's seat would last a month if his careful calculations were correct, so would the four plastic Jerry Cans filled with drinking water.

The overloaded truck groaned when Herman pulled over to refill his road bottles at the last cold beer bar on the laterite road climbing to the Plateau where roads as such would disintegrate into tracks of churned up sand. On his way inside the sweltering, tin roofed, park bench green buvette, Herman passed an old mama resting her bones on a roughly hewn wooden bench smoking a clay pipe. He tried out a common Libreville greeting that originated with the northern Fang tribe, *"Mbolo."*

"Anh," she nodded. Her caramelized eyes closed to slits. *"Ici on est Batéké. On dit omenizegwa. Ça veut dire, Tu es la?"*

The bridge engineer struggled to imitate the old woman's sing song tone. *"Anh, Way-minis-igua.* Quand j'arrive au Plateau je vais dire Way-minis-igua à tout le monde. Way-minis-igua.*"* The old woman reacted with a disapproving wince. Herman spoke in the painfully enunciated drone of VOA Special English. *"Tu es la ? Ça veut dire quoi, mama-o ?"*

Releasing a good-natured shriek, she puffed on her pipe and replied, *"Je ne te comprends pas, monsieur !"*

A tightly woven pannier, jammed to overflowing with bananas, sat in the dirt propped against the bench instead of riding on her back while she rested before the long trek home. A hand-woven basket bigger than a blond sheepdog, the pannier contained an entire regime of bananas, two hundred of them at least, bright yellow, spilling out of the split liana cornucopia.

The old woman, black coffee skin drooping like tobacco in a drying barn from her slender bones, watched Herman study the bananas then counseled him in broken French that a regime of ripe bananas might be the perfect gift for inhabitants of any one of a dozen remote Plateau villages.

"One cannot grow bananas like these up on the Plateau," she boasted. "One can have this regime to give as a gift for only two-thousand CFA."

After considerable haggling, Herman wrangled the price down to five hundred, then paid her fifteen hundred, tipped her with a green bottle of water pail chilled beer and thanked her for the regime of perfectly formed, six inch long, canary yellow fruit.

After stashing beneath bedding piled on the front seat the frosty beers he had stopped for, Herman lashed the regime of bananas to the Okoumé planks, protecting them from the blistering sun with a green tarp. He felt good, very good and anxious to tackle the Plateau sands.

Just past the Akeni airstrip where the red laterite road bifurcated—a Pygmy village named Oss'Kama to the left, the sprawling Plateau Batéké to the right—Herman climbed until treetops below resembled a gigantic trampoline. Seconds after the road leveled out at the summit, it disintegrated into a pool of deep white sand, a soberingly abrupt quagmire stretching for half a kilometer.

Jacques, the SOLOGAB project manager, had warned Herman that any driver who got stuck in the first trap had no business attempting the rest of le Plateau. Herman rapidly shifted the Land Cruiser into four-wheel drive, highside, dropped into second gear and began to grind forward, careful not to chew down into the sand and high center his vehicle. Felt like farming, plowing a muddy field in spring, that first time through the dry sand at the end of the laterite, Herman's Toyota rafting across a bottomless mire of grit.

By the time he reached the relative safety of hard packed sand, scrub grass and termite mounds on the other side of the trap, Herman's shirt was soaked with sweat. He shifted into third and picked one of four sets of tire tracks disappearing at different points over the broad hill ahead. Then he reached for a beer and dug out his Swiss Army knife, but before he could open the brown bottle, loose hillside sand wrenched the steering wheel from his hand.

Quickly shoving the bottle between his legs, Herman downshifted and floored the foot feed, roaring slowly forward, whipping the wheel a full ten hours, from seven o'clock to five, just to maintain a straight course.

As quickly as the deep sand appeared, it vanished. Then suddenly, the tracks vanished. Then the hill vanished. Herman rolled across a grass plain, picking up speed until he could shift out of four-wheel drive and pop into fourth gear. At forty-five kilometers per hour, Herman relaxed, eased the cap off his sweating beer and hoisted a celebratory swallow.

Peering around the upright bottle, Herman spotted several sets of tracks headed toward a small grove of trees in the distance. Two hundred meters opposite the grove, he spotted more tracks ripping sand from the side of a treeless hill. Hoping to avoid more treacherous powder, he chose to enter the trees, rocking into position over hub deep ruts like a slot car.

No more did his eyes adjust to the grove's cool shade than his front end dropped into a black mud hole. Before the rear tires hit bottom, he slammed the truck into four-wheel again and smacked the transmission stick up into third with a cocky smirk.

The Toyota bogged down. Herman pulled the stick into second and gunned the diesel motor, clenching the wheel and straining his back as if pushing from inside the cabin. Roiling mud wound like an ebony snake through the bosquet. It was clear from errant tracks that other drivers had attempted to escape the morass by hopping out of the ruts to mow through vines and vegetation, only to be forced back into the water trap by trees too big to bulldoze.

When he finally emerged from the ordeal in the dark bouquet, Herman stopped the truck, got out with the remainder of his beer—much of it had spilled into his lap—and scanned the horizon for another set of tracks to follow. There were none, at least none his untrained eyes could see. A filthy patina of muck and mud clods coated the Land Cruiser. Herman checked the ropes lashing his gear, his supplies, his regime of yellow bananas. Reassured that all was well, he finished the beer and set off over the next hill, which could have been the edge of the world for all the chastened American explorer knew.

Twenty minutes later, Hermann wrestled the pickup down a steep slope of sand, white as Arctic snow. Slowing in the valley below, he admitted to himself for the first time that he would be hard pressed to retrace the route he had just taken. Everything appeared starkly foreign yet strangely self-similar. Sand and scrub trees, termite mounds under a blue sky that reminded Herman of the Atlantic Ocean.

On his only other trip out to the tiny village of Ali-Ga, Jacques had joked that it was impossible to get lost on the Plateau.

"It is just too small. So, keep driving," said the red-faced Frenchman, "Someone will eventually see your truck and try to wave you down for a ride."

The only map of the area available for non-military use provided Herman with general orientation. He wanted to head north, taking care not to drift east across the unmarked Congo border.

Herman's blue eyes scanned the bowl-shaped ridge far above the sand valley, two hundred seventy degrees from southwest to southeast. He quickly estimated there were at least forty, maybe fifty, separate sand tracks pouring like sugar down into the bowl where they funneled through treacherous sand pits into a single, unmistakable route marked by ruts carved deeper than the bottom of his door.

Herman had no choice but to drive straight into the maw of a gigantic beast gulping a river of sand through a narrow bottleneck. By far the worst section of road he had yet seen, an isthmus of sand bordered by two tiny streams took opposite routes around the foot of a small mountain looming up ahead, due north in the direction he had to go. Passage, thought Herman, seemed all but impossible.

The Land Cruiser groused and bucked in low gear; the steering wheel pulled against Herman's strong arms. The sand river grabbed hold of the truck and tried to pull everything under as it swept Herman between the narrow streams causing the bottleneck. The sand current pulled him past another shady grove, a tiny mud hut built there, mangy chickens pecking the earth in search of insects, a bramble fence festooned with red flowers.

Suddenly, he foundered in a breathtaking cataract of wild, desperate tire tracks circling, spiraling, gulping other tracks splattered across a turgid white sand lake ringed with trees.

Before he could react to the undertow, Herman felt the truck sink, fight the current and sink again, a panicked elephant in quicksand. Herman slammed the shift lever into reverse, felt the load buck as the Land Cruiser lurched backward and clawed deeper. Before the desperate cycle repeated itself, Herman stomped on the clutch pedal. The entire Plateau seemed to shudder, and the Toyota came to a jarring halt.

Herman grew up in rural Iowa. He spent two years in Togo as a Peace Corps volunteer building spring boxes. He knew about mud. To compensate for his lack of experience with sand, he applied what he knew about mud. It took him two hours to dig beneath the wheels one at a time, replacing sand with wood he chopped using his digging tool, a broad machete. Took him easily another thirty minutes to excavate the high centered front and rear axles. He scattered branches and vegetation ten meters in front of the truck then knocked the top off a sand hill blocking the driver side door and took his place in the pilot seat where he promptly guzzled a sweating beer. Inhaling a deep, frustrated breath, Herman pushed the stick into second gear. He calmly rolled off the platform of sticks and back into the raging chaos of white sand.

He stomped the accelerator. The engine screamed. He pushed and pulled and crushed the pedal into the floorboard. Bone wrenching torque, God awful heat, unmitigated horsepower, it frightened him almost as much as the possibility of deadly serpents lurking in the brush he had cut down to facilitate his escape.

When at last the extraordinary truck waded ashore on the other side of the sand ocean, Herman felt as though nothing could stop him. He double clutched, eased the Land Cruiser into four-wheel low in anticipation of the uphill slog ahead, then shifted into third for the first time in a long time. In a heartbeat, conditions changed again. He downshifted and accepted the fact that he had committed himself to a deeply worn track while three newer traces curved out of reach in three different directions. Two or three seconds later, he hit the foot of the hill. The nauseating chug, bite, dig cycle that sank him in the sand ocean threatened to mire him all over again on the hazardous slope. Herman hammered the hi-lo shift lever back into high and floored the accelerator, talking to himself the way a Kamikaze pilot might, threatening to incinerate the powerful diesel before letting up on the foot feed short of the summit. Determined to prevail, there was little work to do but mash the accelerator fiendishly, throttle the steering wheel without mercy and try to relax while clawing up a sand hill so slowly the speedometer barely bobbed above zero.

Little by little, belying the deafening roar of the motor and the rising heat gauge, Herman scaled the giant hill. Soon, the entire valley, all of its sand scars funneling into the bottleneck leading to the treacherous sea of sand, became visible. The ascent seemed to take an hour but only nine minutes elapsed on the way to the summit where Herman's gasping truck churned through foot deep sand, but sand with a distinctly solid bottom. Sinking out of sight was not a problem as the truck crawled past a dozen or more alternate tracks flowing into the central artery from either side and plowed around small plots of spindly manioc where scrawny goats nested upon mounds of sand blanketed with black goat pellets. He inched past three short, muscular women trudging shin deep through sand, panniers heavy with manioc and firewood strapped to their muscular, bare shoulders, still more firewood piled on their heads.

Stuck in first gear, the motor wailing, Herman entered a village of mud huts constructed along the eroded banks of a wide swamp, muck brown sand splattered with heel prints. He had reached Otou, the first Plateau village, the one closest to the laterite road he had left hours earlier.

Nearly noon, a hundred or so tin roofed mud huts baked under merciless equatorial sun. When Herman's Land Cruiser bogged down in the center of Otou, he bumped the four-wheel drive lever into low without hesitation. Seemingly unstoppable, the HJ-47 crawled at a snail's pace through the village, giving the American civil engineer plenty of time to study each dwelling, undulating walls of ocher mud applied to slender poles and vinous wattle. Visible through yellow mud piled at the base of the walls on a number of older huts, fragile, rotten wood skeletons crumbled under the weight of the mud. Dark windows, almost paranoid in smallness, denied him any view inside the shuttered huts.

Otou appeared deserted. With the exception of a few stray goats, black chickens and the women Herman had seen earlier, the only sign of life were the human tracks sculpted in the turgid surf of dirty sand. Up ahead, the road cornered abruptly to the right. A young girl darted from a black doorway towing a heavy bundle tied in red cloth. She planted herself in full view of the screaming, slow motion truck, stuck out her arm slightly above horizontal and began to wag her hand from the wrist fitfully as a cat's ear. She wore a powder blue dress; one any Iowa schoolgirl might own were it not so stubbornly clean and threadbare. Cinched round her narrow hips, a cotton pagne smeared with dark paisley on a yellow field reached down to her skinny shins. Her black legs were spindly, scarred with abscesses and accidental machete wounds. Her bare feet floated on top of the sand, big toed, calloused, flat. The sand current pulled Herman directly alongside the girl, close enough he realized she was groaning loudly, a plaintive monosyllable that reached an intense crescendo as he passed, *"Anhhhhhhhhhhhhhhh!"*

Once around the crook in the road that pointed him east toward a lush bosquet paved with black soil, real dirt dotted with tiny wild pineapple jewels, his eyes fell upon a mud hut just like all the other mud huts of Otou except for careless brush strokes of violet peeling off the door. Crude whitewash symbols decorated both jambs. He saw the word "Restaurant" carved into the mud below a wood shutter and immediately pulled to a stop in deep sand out front hoping to find a warm beer and a cold lunch inside.

Herman's eyes adjusted slowly from the blue Plateau sky to a termite mound brown interior revealing a main room roughly two-thirds the size of the small hut. A dark blue cloth pagne curtained off an exposed wattle hallway visible below the drape. *"Allo?"* he called cautiously. *"Manger-manger? Allo? Weimenizegwa?"*

Out front where the Land Cruiser's hot metal crackled and popped, a girl with a shrill voice shouted something in Batéké. Herman thought he heard a name spoken in the flurry of Bantu, "Berthe!" and moments later a pregnant, bare shouldered woman wrapped in an elaborate green, yellow and red pagne bearing the portrait of the Pope swept aside the blue curtain and sidled into the cave. Still a teenager, Herman guessed, Berthe's welcoming smile whetted the engineer's appetite. Cinched tightly to her husky back in a swath of Pope cloth, a tiny baby struggled to hold its head erect in spite of the rhythmic bobbing of the mother's bare feet on the pounded earth floor.

Herman again used the greeting he learned from the old mama who sold him the regime of bananas, *"Weimenizegwa."* The pregnant woman's eyes dilated into large black pearls. Herman mimicked eating with two fists. "Manger?"

"Anh!" she smiled to cloak her embarrassment and fumbled with limited French, *"Viandes?"*

"Bière aussi ? Anh ?"

"Oui monsieur, bière aussi." The young woman bowed politely, turned to leave then stopped to pull a broken-backed chair clear of a handmade wooden table and waved for Herman to sit.

Herman felt his own cheeks blush. *"Merci, madame."*

Several minutes passed, long enough for the thirsty American to notice sweltering heat radiated by the low roof tin. He began to wonder if his request for beer had not been understood. He cleared his throat and was about to call Berthe by name when the youthful voice out front screeched again, again saying something incomprehensible to Herman except for the word *"bière,"* which possessed an unmistakable ring. Almost immediately, a small boy appeared balancing a dripping wet brown bottle and a chipped drinking glass on a faded red plastic tray.

As if performing a ritual dance, the child, no older than seven or eight, swept off the table with the side of his small hand then fussed with the placement of the beer bottle and glass, reminding Herman of his father's dog Hap who circled and pawed his bed endlessly before lying down. The tiny waiter dug into the pocket of his tattered short pants, produced an old-fashioned church key and wrestled off the bottle cap with a look of such profound concentration that Herman could barely stifle a laugh. The boy finally cracked a smile and slowly tilted the chipped glass to minimize the head as he poured sudsy, warm beer. Then he scurried over to the blue curtain where a black hand passed him a bowl of water sharing a metal saucer with a cracked wafer of worn yellow soap.

Herman washed his fingertips like a priest before Communion and gulped down a glass of beer, then another. The beer and the intense heat flooded his brain with momentary giddiness. He slowly poured a third glass in the style of the young waiter. When he glanced up again, he found a young girl's almond shaped, nut-brown face floating in the small front window next to his table. Flawless white teeth and lively eyes brightened the room. Herman recognized her as the girl with the bundle he had passed by. He winked and practiced his one word of Batéké, *"Weimenizegwa."*

"Anh!" beamed the girl in the powder blue dress. *"Vous parlez notre langue bien, monsieur !"*

"Merci," he said, nursing his beer with increasing uneasiness under the girl's relentlessly invasive gaze. Berthe finally returned with three white enamel bowls balanced on a glass plate frosted opaque from years of washing with sand. Just like the boy who poured the beer, Berthe fussed with the dishes until she discovered some arbitrarily correct placement. Once satisfied, Berthe sat across the room next to another small window. The girl in the powder blue dress quickly joined her and the two young females chatted in Batéké while Herman circled his meal. A large bowl overflowed with manioc the color of dishwater, a sticky, grayish staple shaped like a French baguette. A middle-sized bowl contained legumes; smoked termites no bigger than burnt match heads floated in fluorescent orange palm oil glazing a veritable swamp of bright green grass. The smallest bowl was reserved for the main meat course, a shattered bone about two inches long, three-eighths of an inch in diameter, spearing two ounces of gazelle foreleg, fur and all, drizzled with a watery au jus.

Herman stabbed a chunk of manioc with his bent fork, dipped one corner into the legume, a toe in an icy pond, and took a nibble. The cloying flavors and vinegary aromas, though almost pleasant, assaulted his senses. He chewed like live snakes filled his mouth and quickly cleared his fork of manioc to attack the gazelle. Then, changing his mind, he seized the bone in his fingers. The delectable gazelle meat suffered from the pervasive pungency of tripe soaking in saltwater.

Herman dunked another wad of manioc into the brown sauce and shoved it into his mouth. Berthe and the girl in the powder blue dress watched his every move, every reaction to the strange flavors he washed down with generous gulps of warm Régab.

"Bien," he muttered. Both windows framed razor bald, wide eyed children watching Herman eat. He grinned stupidly and said, "Bien-bien-bien."

When Herman finished eating, Berthe and the girl in the powder blue dress approached his table. *"Tu vas à Ali-Ga?"* the girl asked.

Herman answered, "Oui."

She smiled shyly, looked at her feet, *"Amenez moi?"*

Berthe smiled. *"Amenez, amenez, monsieur, s'il vous plait. Merci?"*

Unable to refuse, Herman smiled. *"Bon. D'accord."*

The Toyota growled and gripped deep. Sitting forward on the edge of the passenger seat, the girl—Elaine was her name—waved to excited village children through the side window. Elaine's heavy round bundle tied in red cloth rode atop a jiggling case of warm beer in the back. Herman shouted a final word of thanks to Berthe who cradled her complimentary bunch of unbruised bananas the way doctors deliver newborns. The boy-waiter—Berthe called him Bobo—held out his little hand palm up and shouted over the sound of the diesel, *"Pamé adoro!"*

Herman looked over to Elaine for a translation. "He asked you for money. Don't give it to him," she advised solemnly as the powerful truck chewed into the sand and crawled away.

The small bosquet at the east end of Otou, dark with thick leafed trees, momentarily bathed Herman's truck in cool shade before the black dirt track petered out and the thicket, studded with pint sized pineapples, dissolved into sun baked manioc fields. On the right, a dozen shirtless, ebony skinned men toiled to secure ten-meter metal roof sheets to stout wooden trusses balanced on a recently finished masonry shell. Next to a rumbling, cement encrusted mixer stood a short white man, bearded blond, his hair tressed in corn rows, and an even shorter black girl with a matching hairdo. Together, they watched Herman's truck plow through sand chewed up by a Land Cruiser parked at the school work site, an old, beat-up HJ-45 with a Peace Corps logo on the door.

The white man resembled the boy waiter in that his shirtless, meatless torso featured a pronounced belly pot that disappeared into tattered short pants. He and the girl watched without expression as the truck labored past. Once it became clear that Herman was not going to stop, the couple began to wave furiously.

"Là c'est qui ?" Herman asked.

"Là c'est Monsieur Bob et sa femme, Sophie," Elaine replied. *"Ils se marient."*

Sometime after the school building disappeared from Herman's rear view mirror there came a faint but determinedly shrill cry from Sophie, which fell silent only after a considerable statement. The Toyota groaned. Seven beer cases chattered. Herman quickly maneuvered to jump from the set of deep tracks he was trapped in to a newer, shallower set Elaine had pointed out. Then all of a sudden, Elaine erupted in reply to Sophie's communiqué, her close shaved head bobbing up and down.

Herman barely heard Sophie's response over the roar of the truck. But Elaine heard it. "Anh!" she purred before launching again into a lengthy response to the wife of a Peace Corps volunteer now standing hundreds of meters to the rear.

In spite of Elaine's distracting presence, the rigors of Plateau driving demanded Herman's full attention. The sand leading to Otou prepared him for tracks appearing out of nowhere and disappearing just as quickly. Deep sand rivers drained into dark, wet bosquets, which in turn dissolved into steep uphill challenges. Seemingly endless plains dropped off precipitously where unseen streams gouged out breathtaking valleys.

Rounding the rim of a particularly stunning canyon, the bridge engineer made rapid span calculations without even thinking. He slowed down where his line of sight grazed the top of a tree and fell unobstructed to a riverbank far below. Trigonometry raced through his head, estimating that the valley floor lay at least half a kilometer from his precarious position sideways on the steep hillside. The heavily loaded Land Cruiser listed a good twenty degrees into the elliptical canyon bowl, which he measured to be at least three kilometers across the long radius, and another two kilometers, according to the odometer slowly ticking off the distance he traveled, across the short radius.

Herman's heart pounded. He visualized a span arching gently upward à la Robert Maillart, the Godfather of modern concrete spans. Like Maillart's delicate Alpine roadways, Herman's approach would follow the curve of the canyon rim. He would tilt the bridge deck to add strength and beauty to a rising arch while requiring traffic to slow down and observe the cornucopia spilling out flora and fauna beneath his wondrous concrete sculpture.

"Monsieur Hair-mann, on y va ?" Elaine interrupted Herman's reverie timidly, craning her thin neck in the general direction of Ali-Ga, pointing with her chocolate lips and chin.

Herman drew in a deep breath of air fecund with opportunity. *"Oui,"* he sighed, releasing the clutch slowly on the perilous traverse contour of the breathtaking canyon, *"on y va."*

He pulled a warm beer from behind the seat and handed it to Elaine, fishing for his Swiss Army knife and downshifting at the same time. Without prompting, Elaine shoved the bottle top into her radiant smile and wrenched off the cap with her teeth, her body quickly recoiling from the warm, frothy mousse, passing the slobbering bottle back to the driver at the end of a long, thin arm. Impressed, Herman boasted in French, "I'm going to build a bridge like you have never see, Elaine!"

"Oh," she replied nonchalantly, "I have seen many bridges."

"But not my bridges," he countered.

"But I have seen you," Elaine interjected coyly, "at Green River near Claudette's Magic Lake. I was there when you and the fat Frenchman visited the site for the new *goudron* and the *pont* that will connect Ali-Ga with Oss'elli."

"That fat Frenchman is my boss! You were there? All I remember are the boys standing up in their little pirogues."

"I was doing laundry, on my way back from the plantation my brother Fidel cleared last dry season. You and the fat Frenchman argued like two old women, that is what Chef Albert said after you left. Why don't you want to build the bridge near Magic Lake?"

"Because I want to build it farther downstream, so village life won't be disrupted. I do remember seeing girls doing laundry, and kids bathing, and women collecting drinking water and fishing. You don't want a bridge to cross right there do you? That would ruin everything."

"But if the road does not come through the village, then the village will have to move to the road. That is what Chef Albert told us. Green River swims through twelve lakes around Ali-Ga. We will find another beach to wash our dishes. It would be better than moving the village"

"Twelve lakes?"

"Yes. One of them is mine, or it will be when my grandmother dies. Then they will call it Elaine's Lake and all the fish, and all the water will belong to me."

"Really?"

"Oui, c'est vrai," she smiled.

"What will you do with your own lake?"

"I will give it to my daughter."

"You don't have a daughter!"

"No, but I will soon enough. If you hire my boyfriend Yves to work on your bridge, then he will give me a baby."

"How old are you, Elaine?"

"I'm going to be thirteen."

"That's too young. What about school? Do you go to school?"

"Yes, and if Yves doesn't give me a baby soon, the school master, Monsieur Godefroid, will expect to sleep with me when I am thirteen."

"That's terrible!"

"Non." Elaine just laughed and pointed to a barely visible sand track climbing the side of a treeless hill. "Go that way past the old village Okouya, you'll avoid Louis's terrible road."

"Who is Louis?"

"He is the youngest son of Chef Albert's youngest wife. Louis drives for Edouard Mbadou. He wants everyone to call him *É'choué*. It means, 'Let's Go.' Last year, Louis drove the soccer team to a bosquet over there where we were headed. It took them all day to chop a road through the forest. Louis boasted his road would cut thirty minutes off the trip to Akeni, but it actually adds an hour even if you don't get stuck. We call Louis's Road the Thirteenth Lake. You will meet Louis. He tells everyone that he will be your captain because he has a license to drive."

"Don't worry, Elaine, I will decide who works for me, not Louis, though a man who can drive might come in handy."

"Louis also says that you will hire his girlfriend Babette to be your housekeeper and cook."

"It sounds like Louis has me all figured out."

"Not Louis, Babette. We call her É'choué's brain. All the men want to sleep with her, but she told me she wants to sleep with you and then she will be your femme like Sophie is Monsieur Bob's femme. And you will give her a gift, a *metisse* baby, and new dresses, and a cement house with a tin roof." Elaine bubbled over with laughter.

Herman hesitated, unsure what to say next. "I came here to build a bridge, not to find a wife, Elaine. But I will need a housekeeper. Would you be interested?"

Elaine's eyes expanded to the size of saucers. "Oui, Monsieur Herman!"

"You will have to stay in school, and no babies, no sleeping with le maître either. I could pay you two thousand CFA per week."

"Oui, Monsieur Herman! Take that track over there, it looks bad but it's very fast."

As promised, the road chosen by the precocious twelve-year-old in the smiling powder blue dress quickly delivered Herman to the idyllic, palm tree lined, brown mud village of Ali-Ga without further surprises. The differences between Ali-Ga and villages closer to the hard road and commercial centers like Akeni were striking. Ali-Ga was much cleaner, much prettier, its houses better maintained and roofed in thatch instead of rusting tin or blinding aluminum tôle.

Surprised plantation women and children, many of them naked, reacted to Elaine's excited shouts by trotting behind the truck through the sand swamp bisecting Ali-Ga. Herman stopped at the center of the village near a palm tree toppled and tapped for its sweet wine. Anyone not out farming, fishing, washing laundry or hunting assembled around the truck. Herman estimated that at least ninety men, women and children pressed close to watch him slip out of the truck and shake old Chef Albert's withered, black hand.

"Weimenizegwa, Chef." Herman's greeting provoked a round of raucous laughter from the villagers.

A tall, lanky African, cock sure of himself judging by his dilatory gait, stepped forward and gave Herman's hand a limp shake. *"Bienvenu, Monsieur Herman. Je m'appelle É'choué-Louis."*

"Glad to meet you, Louis. Elaine has told me you know how to drive," Herman replied in a deliberate effort to mask his instant contempt for the ingratiating smile wrapped three-quarters of the way around É'choué's face.

"Oui, Patron. Je suis à votre service !" The Chef's youngest son reached into the crowd and pulled Babette forward. Herman immediately remembered her from his first trip. A disarmingly voluptuous teenager, Babette possessed uncommon beauty, flawless, smooth mocha skin, glistening tresses studded with blue beads, and lips, ruby red like the tail of the grey parrot prominent upon an expensive Dutch Wax pagne cinched beneath Babette's muscular, bare arms and shoulders.

Jacques, the fat Frenchman, had pointed out Babette to Herman when they visited the proposed Green River bridge site, slapping the top of his fist with the palm of his opposite

143

hand to convey a sudden urge to copulate with her. Louis didn't seem to notice Herman's momentary lapse into a fantasy involving Babette's high cheek bones and creamy eyes. "You will need a housekeeper," Louis said. "If I may present Babette."

"That's all right, Louis. I appreciate the offer, but I've already asked Elaine to be my housekeeper." Herman couldn't decide who appeared more devastated, Babette or Louis. Hoping to alleviate their obvious embarrassment, he pushed through gawking villagers to the rear of the truck, where Elaine, after fighting through the crowd, joined him. "I brought you a cadeau," Herman announced, lowering the tailgate, "from down in the forest, a regime of bananas."

As if an unfelt wind suddenly sucked all the monotony out of the village, a collective gasp went up and the crowd condensed into a knot of expectation. Herman threw off the tarp and hoisted the huge regime of ripe bananas over the side, gently lying it on the sand at Chef Albert's feet. Herman made a sweeping gesture to indicate that the bananas were for everyone. Now it was the Chef's turn to act embarrassed. The confused village elder nodded as if he understood his new role as dispenser of bananas. Then, with a wave of his hand, the Chef abdicated all authority.

A riot erupted immediately. Men, women and children dove for the yellow regime. No holds were barred. Women clawed the children. Men elbowed women out of the way. Old pounded on the young and the young kicked and bit and scratched their way through the tangle of dark limbs to get one of the rare forest bananas. Soon, victorious villagers began to emerge from the melee clutching handfuls of smashed bananas.

A tenacious few villagers remained locked in mortal combat over the last pieces of fruit clinging to the main stem that resembled the broken spine of an antelope long dead. Deeply distressed by what he had just witnessed, Herman waded in and began pulling away youthful bodies. On top of the pile, he found Babette, her face clawed and bloody. Next, he untangled the powerful arms of a muscular young man he would later name as foreman or capitaine of his survey crew, Elaine's brother Fidel. Fidel had a bloody lip. Then he pulled off Yves, Elaine's boyfriend, also young, husky and bruised. Finally, Louis, É'choué.

Louis's ear, split with teeth marks, bled freely. The flesh surrounding his right eye, badly swollen, burned redder than pili. Louis rolled off to the side. Herman felt woozy. He could plainly see Elaine's powder blue dress stained with blood. Her chocolate face had paled. Head to toe, her tiny body was bruised and scratched. Blood trickled from the corner of her mouth. Barely conscious, murmuring half delirious nonsense, Elaine had stopped smiling.

At a loss for words to convey his disgust, Herman grimaced at Chef Andre. *"Pourquoi?"* he bellowed angrily, spinning around to beseech the villagers, many of them wearing foolish grins.

Louis took it upon himself to speak for the crowd. "The regime of bananas, patron, we do not often see so many forest bananas here on the Plateau."

"You fight over them? Look at all of you; look at Elaine! Put her in the truck." Herman spat out the command with unambiguous outrage, "NOW! Where is the nearest hospital?"

"Akeni," Louis groaned. "Can I go too? I'm hurt, patron."

"You can ride in the back. Move it! Let's go!"

Louis halfheartedly joined Yves and Herman as they pushed Elaine across the front seat until her head rested in Fidel's lap while the villagers chanted with collective urgency, *"É'choué!"*

10. Crazy Joseph

When Claude Emmanuel Mpo's brother, Joseph Désiré, returned from a weeklong symposium on African socialism in Arusha, Tanzania, he found a brand-new Land Rover parked beside his house. School boys scuffled for the privilege of washing the beautiful truck and caressing its bright green paint. By overloading the roof rack until the springs flattened and the frame rested on the axle, Joseph Désiré was able to transport every beer cassier belonging to the villagers of Imiga. So began, with a small green four by four, Imiga's wholesale beer business. The Land Rover came with the elected job of Président de l'Assemblé d'Akeni, a local government group with the well-deserved reputation of sticking its nose in the business of everyone in the district without providing mandated services. But the likeable Joseph Désiré soon changed all that. He became in fact the most effective Président de l'Assemblé anyone in Akeni District could remember.

Besides making regular beer runs for all the traditional Chefs de Regroupement, Joseph Désiré provided benches and desks for fourteen grass-roofed, mud brick elementary schools that had lacked the fundamentals for decades. When no one else was bold enough to do so, Joseph Désiré fired Jean de Dieux, the mercurial elementary school *maitre* in Imiga who showed up drunk for class every morning and used his *niveau intellectuel* to excuse the fact that far too many of his school's girls had become pregnant. Joseph Désiré stocked the district clinic with aspirin and antibiotics, bandages, sutures, stainless steel surgical tools and a book on first aid written in simple French.

He opened a carpentry shop as soon as beer profits permitted, and the carpentry shop soon began producing chairs, beds and armoires that rural villagers could actually afford. In Akeni District, everyone agreed that Joseph Désiré was a good man who honestly looked after the best interests of his constituents.

Not long after celebrating his fifteenth anniversary as Président de l'Assemblé, a powerful Bapanou sorcerer stopped at Joseph Désiré's office to ask if he might spend the night in Imiga. Though no enemy of the Bapanou, neither was Joseph Désiré a particular friend of his rival neighbors, so he politely refused and sent the sorcerer on his way. That night, Joseph Désiré experienced a painful shift of destiny: he dreamed he would lose his first wife of thirteen years along with his new house and its smooth cement floors, the light bulb in the main room; along with the red Toyota 4-Runner that replaced his exhausted Land Rover; along with the beer business, the carpentry shop; along with the reputation and respect he had earned — all this because he had refused a bed to the Bapanou sorcerer.

Using the new Assemblé truck, Joseph Désiré began collecting junk and surprised everyone by constructing a monumental radio antenna from wood scraps, rope, plastic hose, wire, tree branches, antelope skin and empty sardine cans. When the contraption was finished, Joseph Désiré desperately attempted to contact the Bapanou sorcerer to explain, to apologize.

Day-after-day, he stood in the blazing sun, in the rain, pressing to his mouth a tin funnel wired-up to the antenna with a narrow section trimmed from liana. District residents who once respected him started to laugh, first one, then another, then everyone, even the school children who had grown up calling him Papa Joseph. Someone thought of the unkind name, Zéro, zéro, un: l'Operateur. The moniker stuck. District residents couldn't help but snicker when they heard or spread another rumor about antics of the International Telephone Operator, Joseph Désiré.

Meanwhile, the Akeni Assembly quietly elected a new President. Joseph Désiré seemed oblivious when he lost his truck. Beer transport never resumed. The new President confiscated all the cases and bottles and opened a bar in the back of his house. The carpentry shop closed. The schools fell back into a monotony of disorder, abuse and neglect. Respect for the office of the President evaporated faster than spilt petrol.

Before long, Joseph Désiré stopped wearing clothes, even the second hand, double breasted, beige polyester suit he so loved. Fed up, his first wife finally told him he was crazy. She left, taking his two younger wives with her. Unmoved, Joseph Désiré dismantled his fine house leaving the handmade mud brick for rains to devour, converting the expensive aluminum roof sheets into a scorching metal box where he slept naked on the dirt floor and survived by eating raw termites.

Joseph Désiré started stealing other people's laundry and food. Sometimes he buried it, sometimes he burned it. The villagers of Imiga finally complained to Commandant Mba at the Akeni gendarmerie. They angrily threatened to wedge l'Operateur's foot into a log if the thefts continued. Commandant Mba had greatly admired the former Assembly President and assured the frustrated villagers that the madness would pass if only they remained patient. A short time later, Joseph Désiré attacked Chef Pascal's wife at her manioc pond near Magic Lake, stole the old mama's pannier crammed with tubercles and firewood, and he buried it. With no choice but to arrest l'Operateur for his own safety, the next morning, Commandant Mba persuaded a Yugoslav logger to drive him out to Imiga. A mob of mumbling villagers trotted alongside the Yugoslav's dusty Land Cruiser to the western edge of the village where Joseph Désiré's ridiculous antenna towered over succulent palm trees left untapped ever since madness handicapped their owner. Visible for kilometers around, the ramshackle structure dominated the landscape where a magnificent seven room house with concrete floors and an electric light bulb had once stood.

The crowd approached cautiously. L'Operateur shouted frantically into his tin funnel, *"Allo, allo! Comrade? Allo! A vous?"* Commandant Mba climbed out of the Yugoslav's truck and addressed the defrocked President, gently speaking his name, *"Eh, omenizegwa, papa.* Joseph, Joseph Désiré, you are there?" The cursed man whipped his head around and faced the crowd like a gazelle trapped in a hunting net. Oily tears sweated from his sunken red eyes. Then suddenly Joseph Désiré burst into flame. Commandant Mpo, the Yugoslav logger and the horrified villagers could do nothing but watch helplessly as Joseph Désiré burned until nothing of the poor man remained but rancid ashes.

11. A Message in a Flagon

By I.M. Poe

Nemo me impune lacessit.

I am the unfortunate Fortunato, drawn in wintry irons, with molded granite quartered, and left by Senor Montresor to be soon undone. Certes, my only crime be that of circumstantial acquaintanceship with a madman. The ignominy, suffered, I and my family, in the presence of Montresor, a thousand verbal blessures, too many to parry with heated rebuttal, accumulated perforce as coagulant from a wound does into a black pool beside its poor victim until, at end, the aggrieved vessel is drained of all bloody good.

Having thus succumbed with heavy breath to Montresor's assassinations, and fearing lest he should beset my fair wife or worse, my belovéd children, with wicked *malefactionem*, devised I this plan, this clever carnival revenge. Assured that lunacy and *paranoea* had consumed my cruel associate, and that apace would he no doubt attempt to consummate my fatality in some hideous and craven manner, I donned a stripéd robe and jester's belled cap, imbibed sufficient Medoc to steady my mettle and embarked upon the forfeit to come.

Near dusk, then, this day soon to be my last, did Montresor accost me with such warmth in the plaza that I, for an instant, as he wrung my hands in his icy fingers, mulled absolving the villain from my sharp retribution. Alas, the cask of Amontillado would be his ruination. "Come," bade he, baiting me, "Come, taste my sherry, *mon cher.*"

Deep in the catacombs beneath Montresor's villa, he wearing a black Death's mask and porting a mason's trowel, and I beneath the belled Sacrifice Tarot and in possession of his left arm, we spoke of his precious family. Believing me to be both fuddled and rheumatic, neither my rasp nor my rale, nor the prick-pricking of the bodkin at my wrist contaminated with purulent *bubon* alarméd him that I should seal his fate as he sealed mine. Yes, he, my tormentor, Montresor, he and his entire family, he and his servants, he and his servants' families, he and his neighbors, he and the entire city – my family but recently westered to safety from this *foetid* den – will depart life.

Conclude I now must, as just one brick cataract remains before I am completely blinded.

What? He calls? "Fortunato!"

I do not but reply more. "He! He! He! He! He!"

12. BEZALEL
[beh · zuh · lel]

Young Bezalel sought shade in the date grove where he lifted his heavy woolen robe and relieved himself in the sand. Then, again, he heard the voice. "Make the tabernacle with ten curtains of finely twisted linen and blue, purple and scarlet yarn, with cherubim worked into them by a skilled craftsman."

Bezalel looked around, uncertain, as ever, whether perhaps one of the older men was playing a trick, throwing voice at him from a nearby tent just to watch him tremble, fall to his knees and wait, his lips pressed against the desert, to receive wisdom, intellect, alpha and beta.

Son of Miriam-sister-of-Moses, Bezalel remembered an especially hot and sleepless night when he was just thirteen. The next morning, the desert was cool. And when Moses ordered the boy to build an Ark of acacia wood 2½ cubits in length, 1½ in breadth, and 1½ in height, decorated with angels and covered in gold, he knew exactly what to do. And when the older men who did not possess such knowledge, asked him how he had become enlightened, he told them he had heard a voice.

The voice no one heard, the voice that spoke without words in the same primal language used to utter forth heaven and earth, the sound of it, the storm it caused in young Bezalel's brain, forced blood into his nose and hot sand into his throat. The master artisan had no choice but to listen, to know. The menorah, so complex, Moses himself could not comprehend its construction. And priestly vestments, fine linen sewed with gold threads no one had ever see before. And ritual oils, and bewildering incenses never before touched, never smelled. And silver, and stone. Bezalel sometimes wondered if he, Bezalel, had carved the tablets kept in the Ark.

And as he knelt there, his head bursting with new instructions for the great tent to house the Ark, which he would obediently build, Bezalel, for the first time in his life, heard the other voice, the one that said, "I won't."

13. Snakes & Violets

Pecker Fanger

Mean Merle Earle couldn't afford to be a mean drunk for the simple reason that he hated drinkin-lone. Drinkin-lone, why then he was always awonderin about rattlesnakes and all that there.

But in a crowded bar, elbow-to-elbow with strangers gettin liquored up real good, why Mean Merle Earle would turn into such an obnoxiously friendly good ole boy, most strangers never suspected, least not right off, just how plain o mean o Mean Merle Earl truly war.

Speakin in brittle, elongated tones harder even to understand than when he was talkin sober, why Merle'd start to jackin that red whiskered jaw ahis. Eventually, he'd latch onto some poor, oiled up sap on the stool next to him and ask, Son? What happen you now? Rattlesnake bite off yer Pecker Fanger?

Pecker Finger? they'd surely ask.

Yer Pecker Fanger? Merle would laugh, exposing a grotesque woodlot of brown stumps tumbling inside his milky-pink mouth. Then Merle would shove his right hand into the hand of that perfect stranger, usually in a dank bar reeking of stale beer and dirty ashtrays and squeeze their hand so dang hard why they couldn't help but fondle on the prehensile gap where Merle's index finger had been plucked from its bed in the bones of his first knuckle.

Never failed either, the stranger would demand of Merle, What happen cher finger?

Merle Earle would laugh a little too hard en say, Yer Pecker, son?

Yer Fanger?

Told you, rattlesnake bit on me. No wetback Doc kept acuttin off little pieces mo fanger till this here's all's got me left. Clean cut off yer Pecker, son.

By now, even the strangers Merle got to laughing hard were starting to get a little pissed off. And they'd say, My what?

Merle—as he so often did growing up in the heartbreakingly lonely mountains of western North Carolina, which is where he learned to shoot the eyes out of wild pigs and black bears, which is why a developer in Las Vegas in the 19-and-70s, after Merle ventured out thataway looking for construction work, hired the quote-unquote Crazy Hillbilly Motherfucker to hunt & kill all the rattlesnakes infesting the desert site of a new casino-hotel; which, that is how Merle ended up snakebit on the tip of the right index finger—Merle would stuff his four-fingered right hand down the front of his pants. Then with his good left hand he would, while simultaneously delivering a perversely soul invading Evil Eye, unzip his pants. The tip of his thumb would wiggle out his fly like a scared puppy from under a couch cushion, just barely a nose's worth, and then he'd say, Yer Pecker, son?

O Merle Earle was an inveterate liar. Truth, to Merle, were truth say a bank account, truth was a big, fat, fully fungible slush fund to be nefariously misappropriated. The Pecker Fanger gag most often blossomed into a fraudulent tale of jungle sniping and pillaging villages in Vietnam, raping "there" women, strafing huts filled with screeching children: Guttin live any them Gook ole boys we suspects is Charlie. Merle not only lied, but he took special pleasure in telling sickening lies, shocking, revolting, spine chilling lies. At five feet and six, such lying made him feel tall. Seeing total strangers cringe and blanch and pull away from him, it made him feel tougher than he already war.

True, Merle war a rough customer. But when that one, extremely rare specimen of a drunken stranger failed to withdraw in disgust from one of Merle's faux combat stories, if they actually, you know, moved closer to him, got inside

Merle Earle's lump covered head just a tiny bit, they would more oftennn not pity the goofy ass liar. Merle's charades evaporated like meadow fog, like when the sun come sneaking over the mountain top round noon. Strip him of lies, what was left of Merle was like a mountainside deep in the Pisgah, like fallen poplars rotting on top of forest compost spread a foot thick over water borne, shit colored clay incapable of supporting the heft of enormous green boulders that slowly, slowly slipped inhospitably downhill.

Merle, you see, quit high school in 1970 to enlist in the Army. The recruiter signed him up for Infantry training at Fort Polk, Luzy-ana pending of course completion of basic training at Fort Leonard Wood, Misery. But Merle never graduated from basic. He was just too Gung-Fuckin-Ho, if that be possible. The other recruits, draftees and NGs knew this on the very first day when Merle beat a black, red-haired private named Curly half to death for cutting to the front of the chow line. Try as he could to impress the Drill Sergeants and trainees How Tough He War, no one liked Merle. No one.

Graduation week, Merle found out his MOS had been changed from Infantry to Truck Driver. WHAT THE FUHH!?!? O Merle up and stole four M-16 rifles from the armory and hid them, disassembled, in his bunk and locker. Brigade Commander, Colonel Armitage, called a surprise inspection. And tell you what, when the Colonel found those missing weapons, why he snatched one of Merle's spit shined black combat boots from off the just buffed floor and beat that poor, dumb recruit bloody in the head with it in front of a platoon of privates who'd had to put up with Mean Merle Earle's gooseberry horseshit all through basic.

After the Army booted his ass outta boot camp, instead of going back to the pool table velvet mountain rising up out of the French Broad River valley, Merle went west in search of work. Merle told Toro Weinstein, the developer who first called Merle a Crazy Hillbilly Motherfucker—never to Merle's face mind you—Merle told Toro he'd been an Army sniper. Toro gave Merle a .22 and had him shoot at beer bottles. Merle didn't miss a one, not even the empties Toro tossed into the air. Being a savvy businessman, Toro pointed at the desert and told Merle to find all the rattlesnakes he could, and to kill them. Merle killed eight snakes the first night and thirteen on the second. Toro gave Merle $200, a fifth of tequila and told him to keep hunting snakes.

The next morning, about dawn, half sloshed on cheap tequila, Merle sat down on a rock, put the almost empty tequila bottle behind him and waited for sunrise to bring out the rattlesnakes. He dozed off sitting there, only to wake up with sun scorched cheeks. First thing he did is reach back for the tequila.

Felt me a little prick. Son! Be last little prick I'd go afeelin with that pa-tickler fanger! Fuckin baby rattler not but eight inches long took a chunka me. Blew his fuckin head off right now. Then I crawled the hell outta there on mo achin belly.

For most of the next eighteen months, when he wasn't still too sick to work, Merle labored for Toro Weinstein's construction company. Little by little, a Mexican doctor, Doc Ramirez, who Toro Weinstein paid to take care of Merle's snake bit finger and poison wracked immune system, completely removed Merle's index finger. Then in June of 1972, exactly two years after he'd reported to Fort Leonard Wood, Merle returned home to Chap Mountain minus Yer Pecker Fanger, and a good fifty pounds lighter than when he'd left, but wearing his dress green Army uniform festooned with bogus buck sergeant stripes and a breast pocketful of pawnshop medals including a Purple Heart he'd bought off a down-at-the-heels Las Vegas gambler named Sonny Something-or-Fuckin-Tuther.

When Merle left Nevada, no one said goodbye to him. Nobody ever liked him, not even Toro who only kept him on because the Crazy Hillbilly Motherfucker got rid of all the snakes. Wouldn't fire Saint Patrick, would you?

When Merle got home to Chap Mountain, except for his Ma, nobody come to say Welcome back. Merle had no friends. Not a one. Fact, the only best friend he could remember ever having, Charles Redd from down the mountain, stopped being Merle's friend after Merle whooped Charles in a backyard wrestling match in third grade. Damn near killed Charles, Merle did. Broke the boy's nose, his strumming wrist, and damn near his spirit.

Horsey Meadow

You stand in Horsey Meadow, a deformation of Space Time warped over the knob at the top of Chap Mountain, and you look down the smoky Appalachian valley toward Georgia and Tennessee, and it's like looking through the Hubble Telescope. That's what J.D. Khachaturian thought the first time he stood there in silence a few heartbeats before Sun Fall Set Amethyst Ablaze in Amber Brandy. Time in a Flask, he mused: The History of Earth All Right There. Rushing Away. Slow. I'm HERE, he thought. I Am on The Planet!

Wagoner Schwartz, spiritual teacher in charge of the ten-day Siddhartha-Omni, a spiritual retreat for people like J.D. Khachaturian, people whose means and schedules permitted them to explore catered, alternative religious pathways, placed a paternal hand peacefully on J.D.'s shoulder, nodded reverently and turned back down the path connecting Horsey Meadow with the Pisgah Karmic Studies Center. J.D. stole a last glance back in time as sunlight, like a crazy rat on fire is what it reminded him of, raced back and forth across distant peaks assembled into a non-horizon. In his head, as he turned to go back down to the Center for a two-hour evening session of sitting and silence before supper and silence and sleep, he heard his own voice, which sounded closer to him than he could ever remember in his whole edgy life, say, You some-bitch, yo!

J.D. Khachaturian—the oldest son of a first generation Armenian-American father, a classic traveling salesman who peddled everything from heavy equipment to hard liquor all over the Upper Midwest and both Dakotas, and a Norwegian mother whose father, and uncles on both sides, harvested Taconite from Minnesota's Iron Range—quit his job at Roy's

Mesabi Suds-n-Dog and ran away from home at sixteen. He hitchhiked to New York, bought a plane ticket to Amsterdam, smoked pot for the first time and lost his virginity to a thirty-three-year-old KLM flight attendant. By the time he saw his mother again at his father's funeral twelve years later, J.D. Khachaturian had written music reviews for *Rolling Stone*, *Downbeat*, *The New Yorker*, and a handful of lesser-known magazines. His nightly Memphis syndicated radio show, Bluer Blues, aired on close to one hundred stations across America. He'd appeared on Johnny Carson and Dick Cavett. In 1982, *The Tick of Blue*, a black-and-white film based on J.D.'s brief life before Hieronymus Khachaturian, J.D.'s father, committed suicide, won two Academy Awards, Best Soundtrack and Best Documentary.

J.D. sauntered slowly down the mountain to a split in the meadow grass path–Pisgah Karmic Studies Center, A Sharp Razor Right; To The Left, On Down The On Down The On Down The Mountain. Some-bitch, yo!

Standing at the side of the Chap Mountain road leading to the Center kind of hunched over with a bunch of blue violets in one hand, a long, opaque snakeskin in the other, Merle Earle looked into the eyes of J.D. Khachaturian, expecting them to dart away, afraid, disgusted, uninterested. Whaver, Merle muttered silently to himself.

But J.D., a self-styled music ethnographer who had collected on tape and film songs from every corner of the world, studied Merle carefully, unafraid, unashamed, deeply curious. Merle stood beside a shovel propped up on a pile of mud scooped from a side ditch carrying some small quantity of the copious mountain juices gouging wounds from rock and mud roads before reburying them. It was spring, wet and warm, the two reasons why Merle wore ragged, mud caked coveralls—his only pair—pulled down from his chest and cinched around at the waist as if they weren't coveralls at all but a heavy kilt made from the coarse hide of a mountain mastodon.

Merle, his unshaved mug warped stern, detested the Karmic Studies Center worker ban on speaking during Silent Practice

160

retreats. He nodded nonchalantly, exposing the freckled, saucer size bald spot consuming like a slow burning forest fire his head of greasy, graying red hair. How-do, Merle grumbled, his voice too hoarse from smoking cheap cigarettes to muster a real whisper.

J.D. pressed his palms together as if to pray, smiled broadly and bowed like an Asian monk. Then, before continuing down the long, rutted driveway to the dining room, J.D. scribbled in a tiny notebook dangling from a cord around his neck. He passed the leaf of paper to Merle. *Where I come from people hate only two things, snakes & violets.*

Merle studied the message. Then he felt a shovel handle poke him in the butt.

Dangit, Merle, if you'd quit lollygaggin, hiss-pered Mr. Charles Redd, the Karmic Studies Center maintenance contractor who lived a snaky mile down the mountain with two yellow dogs and an ancient mandolin, you mighta cleaned out that ditch before it gets so dark you can't see the bottom when you fall off the edge and clean down the doggone hail.

The next day after morning meditation and breakfast, Wagoner Schwartz suspended Silent Practice for a two-hour Work Period. J.D. Khachaturian signed up for road maintenance. With a heavy, rusty, hickory handled round point shovel over his shoulder, J.D. hiked out past the rumbling stream where the quarter mile long Center driveway always washed out, then up the rocky hill to the main road. He fell last into a queue of tittering men and women trailing Merle Earle who marched stoop shouldered, a cigarette crunched between his flaccid lips.

Quackin-fuckin Duck Babies, that's what Merle called the Karmic Students. Merle hated Work Periods, period. For one thing, he hated women with shovels, especially middle-aged, big-butted women with long, coarse hippie hair lookin even more like a Witch Broom after a dose of mountain humidity and hard water showers.

Merle also hated the ti-red Mule Shit what come outta Everbuddy's Pie Hoe when the So Calt Wholern Dau Goo

Roo ended Silent Practice. And he hated the Useless-ess Tits na Boar work they performed. Merle could do ten times the worka ten them Bootas-n-Harrikishnas ten times fastern ten times sgood. At's fack.

Merle ordered the Karmic Students to spread out along a fifty-yard stretch of curve where a spring far up the mountain pushed the hill into the road along with every wall of rock or wood ever built to retain it.

Now yuz grab the dummy endda at dare earth sculptizin tool and yuz carve yerself up a slice-a this here side ditch what fills with muck fastern you kin empty it-n-ya carry it ALL THE WAY cross the road-n . . .

At this point Merle always rudely snatched a shovel from one of the students—so happened he grabbed J.D.'s—to demonstrate the proper technique.

. . . yuz give it a healthy flip down the other side. Tryn land it on the roof-a Charles Redd's house iffin ya kin. Merle flung a goober of Chap Mountain muck off the side of the road so far you could hear it whacking treetops below for a full five seconds. Now git ta digging.

Merle shoveled the shovel back at J.D. like a Drill Instructor thrusting a dirty weapon into the hands of a raw recruit. Their eyes met. Merle fished into the ripped breast pocket of his insulated coveralls for a cigarette that seemed to J.D. to float untouched from the rumpled pack up into Merle's puckered lips.

They both spoke at the same time. Merle said, You that fella—and J.D. said, Got another one of those smokes for me, partner?

Wearing a twisted scowl that said I doe lie-ak cigarette moochers, Merle fetched the pack and shook one out for J.D., then shared the blue flame of his Army Zippo with the Duck Baby Moonie. He couldn't help but inventory J.D.'s apparel: expensive hiking sandals, lightweight hiking shorts that looked like they could be turned into an emergency shelter, a 1997 Geko Challenge silk tee, a nice, wide brimmed leather hat the color of tobacco spit, and that dumb ass little book-a-hiz on a sissy ass string round his chicken neck.

Son, whatcha gaa ginst Snakes-n-Vilets? Merle asked.

J.D. inhaled the cigarette like he was copping a hit of primo Jamaican through a Rasta Chillum plugged with a fresh nutmeg nut from Zanzibar, then let the smoke out slow though his nose. He felt positively high. Not me, man. It's my people back home. Minnesota Iron Range. Hibbing. Dylan country. Folks hate two things, Snakes and Violets.

Hawhy?

Well, snakes remind them of Satan. And they think violets are just weeds.

Merle looked at his beat up, cheap ass work boots for a second and thought about haulin offen coe cockin the fucker, or better yet poppin a cap skware inis crookit nose, before looking up into J.D.'s spooky but riveting dark eyes, Vilets ain't weeds. Vilets is little girl flowers.

As if heaven had just cracked open for him, J.D. heard a love song in Merle Earle's words. You just now think of that about the violets and little girls?

Merle puffed up tall and wide, shoved his face close to J.D.'s. Son! I don't have a think what I just said. Them vilets was fer my baby daughter Annette. She be five in Jew-lie.

J.D. arched his eyebrows, Snakeskin for her too, son?

Merle twisted away. Fuuuuh! I hunt me snakes. Got me a whole collection-a skins down the trunk my car. Son's, like this. When I meets me a gal I'm thinkin maybe-a pokin I usually axe her if she'd lie-akt see my snakeskin collection. Show em I ain't scared-a no Devil demons such as Satan.

J.D. considered laughing, but instead stripped his cigarette, pocketed the filter and lunged at the mud ditch with his shovel. I'd like to see that collection myself sometime.

Waa-hell. Mebby at the end a Work Period; before you go back to not talking smore.

J.D. carried a shovelful of muck to the other side of the road and hurled it away like a rattlesnake. Do any music, son?

163

Come ghen?

You play an instrument, sing?

Woa-shit. Me? Son, got me music my bones. Mean Eddy Merle Watson was born et-sakly same time on asame daya Febbary 19-en-49.

One of the female Duck Babies, the attractive mid-thirtyish law professor from Charlottesville, Virginia—her green eyes, mid-Atlantic accent and robustly full figure were the reasons J.D. had picked road maintenance over weeding spinach, which the blonde high school psychologist with the smooth, dark complexion and a red BMW had elected to do—squeezed a shovelful of rocky slime in betwixt Merle and J.D.

Askuse me, gentlemen, she gurgled as ooze slithered slowly off her shovel and down the side of the mountain. I thought this was supposed to be Work Period, not Self Gratification Hour.

Merle and J.D. both winked at the same time, J.D.'s eyeball furtive and smooth compared to Merle's clownish contortion. Saying nothing, Merle wandered around the mud road curve, worried that if he said what he was thinking, or even thought too long about what he was thinking, the green-eyed woman might report him to Lillian, the fifty-one year old, divorced, spiritually driven and generally bemused Director of the Karmic Center, which would be, according to Charles Redd, who got it straight from Janice, the Karmic Center Cook, Merle's third & last strike.

French Broad Boys

The next day, J.D.—who had recently separated from his third wife when his fifth psychiatrist suggested that he resume an earlier regimen of anti-psychotic drugs to cope with the fact that his third wife had begun sleeping in a single bed in a separate room because of his snoring—spent Work Period transplanting red periwinkles with Staley, the green-eyed law professor. So far as J.D. knew, he didn't snore.

Meanwhile, Merle had talked to Charles Redd, the straw boss—Charles Redd, old yellow dog owner, straight backed mandolin player for the French Broad Boys bluegrass band, with a cancer surgery scar from his throat to groin, the man who as a boy Merle had kicked the living shit out of—and Charles told him, Merle, you know that fella you give the cig to? Merle, you ever hear-a Memphis DJ named Bluehound? That's him. He come see me and the boys playin in Black Mountain a few years back. Wrote a nice article on us fer Rollin Stone. That was before he went collecting Jigaboo songs over there in Aferca. I heard he got to drinkin too much that there Hoo Doo Juice. Made him crazy. Come home na straight jacket. Told him Howdy yesterday but speck he don't much remember me. Probably can't remember being here in the mountains before ever even.

Come Work Period, Merle was waiting for J.D. to mooch another cigarette. When J.D. didn't show, Merle had to sneak away from the road ditch cleaning crew, skulk through the honeysuckle patch behind the red barn and creep on down back of the Meditation Hall without either Lillian or Charles seeing him for fear it'd be Strike Tree Fir Shit Sure.

Merle found J.D. kneeling beside that big-chested gal from Virginy stickin red posies in the ground lie-ak they was people's souls or sumpin. Hey! There yar, son. Got chur coffin nail.

J.D., annoyed to be bothered but craving a smoke, reached for the cigarette. Thank-ee, son. Keep this up you gonna addict me these wicked thangs.

Worse thins kin happen. Merle slapped open his Zippo. The lazy blue flame swang down brushin past thick black hair coiled at J.D.'s temple.

Staley, this here be Merle Watson's shadow brother, Merle the Duce. J.D. loved the sound of his newly adopted idiom.

Staley liked it to. She played dumb. Really a Watson boy?

Merle shuffled his feet and looked down the front of Staley's baggy tee shirt. Mean Merle Watson arrived on same day back in forty-nine. Name's Merle Earle. Win mean Merle Watson was no bigger-n hop frogs, he'd play his gi-tarn I'd play mo mandolin with Merle's daddy, Doc. Couple years later Merlen Doc was werld famous billionaires and I was thinkin ta droppin outta schoolt go fightin Veet Naym fer ma country. Which die done.

J.D. dropped his head into the flowerbed, knocking off his leather hat. Moist soil covered his forehead when he rose up beseeching, arms extended. Come ken, son? You played mandolin with Doc and Merle Watson?

Merle slowly bent over his own soccer ball size pot belly, retrieved the hat and studied the subtle piercing around the brim—a fenestration of Fender Stratocasters—before returning it to J.D.'s head. Son, did I say I done what I said I done? I did, din die?

You say you done what you said all right, but anybody record any those sessions, son?

Shore did. Ma sist-Ronny got all the tapes.

Never heard of Little Merle Duce and the Watsons. Might be worth a listen.

Might be. Might be not. Them's rare tapes. Merle was still crippled up from havin polio. Doc, he's blind's a bat's you might know. Enme, I'm shortern o Doc's gi-tar standin up. Just a listen's worth a buncha pesos, Pee-dro.

How much?

Merle thought about it for a second. Take that Stevie Ray hat chores, you kin listen to mo travelin tape long as you want in my car.

J.D. smiled at Staley, stood up, put the hat on Merle Earle's head. Sure enough, as he followed Merle to his car, the inveterate liar transformed into the spittin image of Stevie Ray Vaughn, down to a little tobacco colored Zappa patch on Merle's lower lip, a trivial musical detail J.D. had not noticed until right then.

Merle owned a down at the springs blue Ford Escort measled with cheap body filler and crappy paint. He played a regurgitating cassette—clearly Doc and Merle Watson joined by Little Charles Redd on mandolin from right around the time

Little Merle the Duce had whopped Charles' skinny ass back in third grade—all of ten seconds before the Escort battery died. Just as well. Up at the Center, Lillian sadistically banged a brass gong the size of a UFO with a mallet smooth chunk of Appalachian stump wood signaling the end of Work Period and the resumption of Silent Practice.

For the rest of the day, Merle Earle's purloined tape poisoned J.D.'s Silent Practice. In the Meditation Hall, posing in lotus as a genuinely sensitive ascetic surrounded by skeptical women all looking for just such a guy, J.D. kept thinking about mountain music. After dinner, washing dishes in the kitchen at the deep well slop sink, ample women all around him, smiling to hide their cynicism, fluttering almost, in Silent Practice, spooning leftover lo-fat lintels into Tupperware, shoveling dishes onto shelves, mopping the very floor under his flip-flopped feet, J.D. could focus only on the plot hatching in his head like a baby snake crawling out of a cute little egg shell, a nefarious plot to take ownership of Mean Merle Earl's tape.

On the tenth and final morning of the Silent Retreat, Merle Earle—all git up in his best faux Stevie Ray Vaughn: stovepipe black denims, buckskin vest and that broad-brimmed brown leather hat with the Stratocaster breathing holes J.D. had swapped him for a few fraudulent seconds of Charles Redd jamming on the mandolin with Doc and Merle Watson nigh-on-ta fiddy years back—whispered, his breath repulsive with black convenience store coffee and generic cigarettes and bad teeth, into J.D.'s ear. Son, I kin see you wanna buy them thar tapes I got.

Doing his best to respect the few minutes of Silence remaining before the last Work Period of the Siddhartha-Omni, J.D. nodded YES without looking at Merle.

Wander

Staley drove away in her Explorer, Jens in her BMW, Lindsay and Teresa and Alice and Margaret and Roma in their Corollas and Accords and Volvos and Jettas. J.D. waved goodbye to vanishing possibilities and looked across the Escort's rust pitted roof into Merle Earl's mud brown eyes. How much for the tapes?

Merle had a plan, so he talked real cranky on purpose. Made him sound smart and dangerous. Son, how much what?

J.D. of course had a plan too. He'd yielded to Earthly desire and wasted most of the retreat thinking about those tapes. He talked arrogant-like, impatient, the voice he used on clever village musicians in Cameron, Congo and Kenya. You know what. How much?

Whale that kinda depends, donut?

On whaa?

Falla me.

Follow you where?

Son, you gimme this fine hat. Neigh know I kin truss chew. Kint you juss truss me? I lie-ak you. We gonna do this rat. Gitch yer car.

J.D. owned a mountain climbing Hummer but had driven his Mazda up the lousy Chap Mountain Road to the retreat so as not to appear eco-challenged. But down on the winding highway, J.D.'s jet black Miata proved no match for that Crazy Hillbilly Motherfucker—that's what J.D. kept muttering under his breath as he threw himself into one sharp curve after another—driving the beat up two door Ford Escort. After thirty minutes, right about the time J.D. was ready to break off the chase and drive uninvited up to Charlottesville with his fingers crossed to look for Staley, Merle pulled off the road, no turn signal, and ran into a gas station with a liquor store on the side. He come running out with a handful of Jack Daniels in little airplane bottles.

Dropped two on the passenger seat beside J.D. Using a rehearsed Friendly Tone, he says, Merle does, Son, spot me twenty, will ya?

Twenty dollars?

Kin ya truss a fren fer five minnets? Daynnn!

168

J.D. dug for a twenty. Merle ran back inside and right back out with a fifth of Jack and a big smile. Son, we's almost thar now.

Sure enough, just down the road Merle shoved his arm out the window to signal a left turn into a narrow dirt drive leading to a rundown trailer park two hundred yards off the highway past a stand of scraggly willows and sun scorched locusts. J.D. parked his Miata behind the Escort in front of an old double wide and climbed into Merle's car with his two little bottles of whiskey.

Merle cracked one of his and toasted J.D. Son, you a good old feller. Putter dare!

The two men guzzled Jack and shook hands. J.D., for the first time, realized that Merle Earle was missing the index finger on his right hand. What happened to your finger?

On cue Merle replied, Yer Pecker?

J.D. cracked the seal on his second little bottle of Jack. Your finger, Merle, the one you hold a flat pick with? Gotta be hard playin mandolin without the index finger.

Wah-fuhhh. I don't play no more since I loss ma trigger fanger in Nam. We was out on a searchin destroy mission overn Cambodian cuz I uz tough and wiry en Capn sent me down a rat hole after Charlieen the fuggin tunnel's fuggin booby trapt wiff a dozen pie-zun snakes. Coon shoot fast enough for a little racer fugg jumps rat up en bites me on Yer Pecker.

Your Pecker?

Merle wore a morose mask, slowing refilling J.D.'s empty airplane bottles with Jack from the fifth. He and J.D. lit cigarettes in funereal quiet and polished off each another snort before Merle unbuttoned his black denims and shoved his good hand down inside his pants. Yer Pecker Finger, son! Mean Merle roared with sinister laughter.

After two weeks off his anti-psychotics and ten days of the Siddhartha-Omni, J.D. was getting sloshed. What the fuck ever, man, he said. Listen, Merle, we gonna make a deal for the tape or not? You don't know me, but I have connections. We can both make some scratch if you trust me like you say you do.

Merle shot J.D. his evilest Evil Eye. Son, I garn-tee Ima gonna make some scratch offem tapes.

Let's have a listen. Where are they, in the house trailer?

Not so fast, son. Thain't where you think thar. You kin listen to thisin all go fetch the originals. Gotm buried out back.

You said your sister had the tapes!

She ain't really ma sister. Merle winked lasciviously. Ronny lives a couple double wides down from mean Wander.

Before J.D. could protest, Merle shoved in a cassette and staggered toward the old double wide. Inhaling his cigarette slowly, J.D. closed his eyes and did what he did better than anything else, listened to music. But no more had he lowered himself into a meditation better focused than any he had experienced at the Pisgah Karmic Studies Center, when a strident screech slammed open his eyes.

Merle's wife Wanda stood at the busted screen door yelling, You worfless shee-it! Ah sit in here day-in-in-out takin care yer baby girln you comen drink in the carn fronna me? Whachew think I am, stupid?

Naw, you ain't stupid, Wander. You jess ugly!

Wanda rared back and tried to kick Merle in the face from the listing concrete stoop just as four-year-old Annette stepped out holding a plastic baby bottle filled with Kool-Aid.

Annette! What I tell you bout suckin on that bottle? You a baby or a girl? Now gimme that goddang thang! With a snap as quick as a snakebite, Merle yanked the bottle away from Annette and swatted her butt, sending the little dirty faced blond violet back into the trailer crying. Ens fer you Wander, you juss gettin house. I got workado. Na git for ah slap ya silly! Then Merle ran back and jumped in the car, tossing the baby bottle into J.D.'s lap. That there's fer you, my little girl's baby bottle. That's proof you kin truss O Merle the Duce.

I don't want your daughter's bottle! Merle, we gonna make a deal here or not?

Son, already got ourselves a deal. Here's what we gonna do ... Merle turned the key to start the car. Click, click. No juice.

... Sheee-EEEE-EEEEE! Dayannn! Falla me, son.

Merle grabbed the fifth of Jack and scampered across the gravel into the trees. J.D. hurried after him only to find Merle lying on his back staring up at a sawed-off locust branch a good two inches around and about five feet above the ground. Right under Merle's left eye, right smack on the cheekbone, the branch left a rose oozing blood. Mo-k. Mo-k, muttered Merle, three quarters knocked shitless.

Holy Christ, Merle. Oh, man. J.D. helped Merle to his feet. Oh fuck, man. You better go home. We can do this over the phone, by mail. God, you got a raspberry. You need to lie down. Merle.

Na-ha! We come this far. Na Ima take you overt Ronny's double wyatten Ima sneak backen dig up them secret tapes you want so damn bad. We gotta deal.

Snakes & Violets

J.D. sat on a gravel skinned old fold out couch in Ronny West's thirty-year-old double wide living room. Drawn, dusty green drapes gave the room a murky underwater feel. Little violets, purple, blue and white in teacups and plastic glasses, covered the coffee table, kitchen table and end tables. A sweet-scented candle burned. Ronny, a woman of the sort J.D.'s mother would have described as Rough, sat next to him smoking Marlboros and sipping Jack from an airplane bottle. At forty-three, Ronny, mother of two grown children from fathers she wanted to forget, still looked pretty damn good wearing short cutoff jeans and a tee shirt with no bra.

J.D. swigged whiskey from the fifth and looked her over wantonly. How long you known Merle? Know him when he could still play the mandolin?

Merle? She tittered. Na, I han't known him but since he moved here. Couple years. He says you gonna buy them bluegrass tapes. That right?

Maybe.

Maybe? Again, she tittered. Maybe not?

Maybe.

Merle says you hot to play them tapes on the radio in Memphis. Says you a DJ there, J.D.

Merle said that?

Says you got the big bucks ta pay.

J.D. tittered. Well, that depends.

Ronny put her hand on J.D.'s thigh and slid it up to his crotch. Pends on what?

J.D. didn't answer. He leaned over and gave Ronny a big, wet and aggressive kiss, pulling her tongue from her mouth like a snake from a hole. Then they stripped naked and had sex, all kinds of snaky ass sex right there in the violets. When Merle returned with the tapes thirty minutes later, he walked in on Ronny and J.D. squirming around on that gravel-skinned couch naked as a couple jaybirds, their faces buried in the other's genitals.

Wall shee! Put some damn clothes on, son! Ronny, you kin stay naked cuz Ima gonna throw a first-class hump indayoo heerna minit. Merle, his left eye a classic, near swollen shut black-n-blue-shiner with a bright red rose below it, tossed a zipped tight baggie containing four cassette tapes onto J.D.'s startled lap. That thar be forty grand, mister DJ. Ten-n-ten-n-ten-n-ten, juss lie-ak we greed.

Wha?

J.D. stammered. I didn't agree to pay anything, much less forty thousand. I haven't even listened to these. How do I know they're authentic? No, I have to do my homework. If they're good, then I'll shoot you a price. Maybe we negotiate a little. You get paid. That's how it works.

Merle got mad right off. Wha the fuuu? Wha? You tank Ima some kinda Crazy Hillbilly Motherfucker? Son, I wann my money. I wanna nah! Forty-K. Odd take a check. Mean Ronny headin ta Winston fer the NASCAR openern then hail who knows, mebbe back outta Las Vegas even. Ain't that rat Ronny?

Ronny slapped Merle's soccer ball belly. Thass rat, Merle.

J.D. suddenly felt sick. When he reached for his trousers, Ronny tossed them across the room. Wha chew doin? The poor sap shouted. I gotta go. We can continue this negotiation over the phone.

When J.D. tried to stand, Merle doubled him up with a punch in the stomach. Son, ah won ma money.

J.D. didn't want to laugh, but it squirted out. Doesn't work like that, Merle, he grimaced. You're just plain stupid if you think you can rip me off.

Now mean Merle Earle was real mad, rip snortin, asshole reamin mad. He pointed with his good left hand in the shape of a gun and says, Pop a fukin cap in ya rat now cept thad be murder. Awl git ma rifle money though. Got chur car, yer suitcase, yer billfolden that gold watch.

Incredulous, J.D. cried, You gonna rob me now?

Merle shot J.D. an evil Eye. Son, gonna kill yus affer tall.

Ronny hopped up naked and scurried into a room at the back of the trailer. Merle kicked open a door under one of the violet covered end tables, grabbed a rattlesnake by the head and tossed its thick body onto J.D.'s lap. The angry reptile bit J.D. repeatedly on the thigh and chest before escaping behind the couch cushions. J.D. closed his eyes. He watched the sun sink below the non-horizon from an enlightened mountain top. I'm here, he thought. I'm on the Fucking Planet.

Merle swaggered past the dying man on his way to be with Ronny. Thankee fer the Strat hat, DJ-man.

14. Footnote to Doggerel

"Poetry is not for the faint of heart." [i]

A pril gruel. The steady locomotion of shoveling. Smith O'Connor pried up a heavy seven-inch slice of pure white snow, his mother a Polaroid fading from memory: blue plates of moist angel cake in each hand, a piece for him and one for his dad, father and son having, long-agone, just cleared and spread coal cinders on icy sidewalks. When he might have just as well longed for the past, Smith chuckled at the irony. His father, dead of a heart attack shoveling snow, lay frozen for thirty winters. His mother, herself already five winters iced, fell victim to rotten wires and loose screws.

All night long, from the great deafness of distant, half dead townships, had snowplows grumbled down One-Ten, exploding on the half hour past Gap Tooth and Smith's towering house of forty-nine windows swaddled in blue spruce against the bluff. All night long, the thundering hush of oversized flakes blanketing his long, steep driveway tossed him, turned him, deranging his thoughts into a frosty epic poem sluiced through with a remotely haunting chorus.

The woods are lovely, dark and deep,
But I have promises to keep ... [ii]

Around 5 a.m., Smith's wife Frances slipped back into bed after a trip to the bathroom. A few heartbeats later, short of breath and exhausted, escaped the old poet into a subconscious warren / finds himself in a nanosecond illuminated by the cryptic torch of Dream / what's been hounding him / the wintery months passed since his beloved friend Jakes died in a freakish creek side collision involving young Shadow and a panicked buck with an arrow stuck through its neck.

The wide, ice white riverscape's blinding / when the woman's plaintive grunt / pop, pop, pop. Her broom straw hair splays out from under her bulky camo cap meant to cover little, dried apricot ears. A smirk of terminal clumsiness dimpling her ruddy cheeks, is she shortly and in slowed motion all abumble upon the broken surface of thin ice. Frozen momentarily above frigid black water murkied all the muddier under two feet of regurgitated snowmobile slush, her insulated, duck-colored coveralls wick certain death as she grapples futilely / gravity / for breath befuddled.

As Dream cam claws for a wide shot of porcelain dog / ice chunks yaw inside jagged ice ring where down clad in soggy brown numb, woman has just knifed through / bitterly heaves back the breathlessly cold drink she flogs / pitches albino dog himself into Dream's black deeps.

Massive paws maul the still about the hole. His powerful jaws snap bergs into powder / icicles fanged & snags sugar crusted cuff of dunked woman's durable canvas sleeve. Summoning strength few save said snow colored Dream dog could possibly possess, pulls out the beast drencht drowning woman from the hypothermic slackwaterpool / tows he her hull across skyblue to rusty Dreamer's pickup frozen truck inside ice block aqua sinks / has he / she / is saved / was lost.

Steam as off a stewpot lid hugs her / she slues a quavering arm over Dream dog's sturdy platinum pelt / buries her pearled face in a bush of warm hide swaddling the beast's droopy ears / inhales the unwashed smell of dog brush & bedding / he as always nonchalantly heroic & hungry.

Her lips are thin and stiff and black like his, only terser, the worse, hers, for the fleeting terror of freezing stiff. Granite halos encrust her grateful winter twilight-colored eyes. His are ceramic bowls of wild red honey. Doggoboy detects egg whites and wheat toast in the gaps of the woman's smoke-stained teeth and steals a lick off, he / her paled steel face laps / her / he pelf.

The woman rubs his black nose with hers-o-rosy / purrs, "Goo boy," and tugs open a brass breast pocket whisper / produces a small glass phial and a silver spoon / zzzippers: "Here you go, goo boy," pouring sticky lacquer the color of liquid sapphires, "Lil this'll make you feel real / bring me's back / soon's you awakes / s'spoon here."

Goo boy licks clean the / chomps down on the intricately tooled stemware's silver saucer / bolts onto the ice and vanishes, thought like / clencht fangs clutcht / poof / wakes up dreamt of / poet did? Dog-gone? Verses?

Smith slid his ergonomic orange snow shovel under another half foot of fresh white sod. O, cruel, damn you, April, O. Acting on him like a narcotic, reality distended, the truth left maladroit, the noble Dream remembered felt irresponsible. And that made him feel guilty. He should have known / never in the first place been / better than / on the ice to be below the lock & dam at Dresbach.

His brain chopped sloppy Dream ice, scraping image after image off the pavement, sorting through Facts even as Facts turned fluid. He caught a glimpse of his reflection in a large, vaguely warped window / young and but yet old man hunched over a bent spoon scooping sniffles from a drainage swale.

Head dropped determinedly, Smith shoved wet snow thirty feet across to the neighbor's picket fence, hoisted soup onto a slushy mound, melted down from eight feet to four feet high during a cynical warm snap back in early March. The Dream / poem itself / near dissipated, Smith no longer felt good that his black Border Collie Shadow had goosed open & leapt through the sliding back window / saved from drowning that DNR officer, an unselfish duck woman who simply tried to stop him-Smith from driving out on ice no longer safe even for fishing. He just felt guilty, guilty and stupid; stupid for sacrificing the pickup, which wouldn't be salvaged off the river bottom until barge season; guilty for leaving his white retriever Jakes lying on the front seat wrapped in the threadbare blue dog bone blanket he'd slept with most of his life, already twelve hours dead when ice started to buckle beneath the truck in a bungled attempt at a sea burial that, in bleak retrospect, struck Smith silly as a way to honor a beloved pet, albeit a water-loving pet, selfish, impetuous, immature as any puppy love ever / up bolts old poemsmith / Frances, beside herself-half-asleep-worried-sick about Smith, stirs and murmurs, "Wass bride lied?" Silvered spoon is a tongue of flame / igneous in black Shadow's snowy maw clamped / champs hero hard down on darkness. Smith momentarily caresses Frances' warm fingers, like a poem a soft dog ear / tries to say, "Good night, my love," how every night he does, but instead says "Goo bye, my Wolf,"/ iii / when Smith his chest has clutcht, and as loudly can only grouse, "Promises, I kept!" just as the tumult of snowplows tumblt past.

---

i *I Remain, The Letters of Lew Welch, Vol Two*, (Grey Fox Press, 1980). Letter fragment, Welch to Elspeth Smith, June 1969. Welch vanished without a trace in 1970.

ii "Stopping by a Woods on A Snowy Evening", <u>New Hampshire</u>, Robert Frost, (Holt, 1923). In December 1962, Frost suffered a severe heart attack and died in January 1963.

iii *Doggerel, Posthumous Collected Love Poems*, Smith O'Connor, edited by Dr. O. Frances Margarita, (Trumpet Tear Editions, 2020). Author of many books, he is best known for retelling the Orpheus & Eurydice myth in <u>Pearl</u>, an account of his missionary daughter's abduction by a rebel warlord in Eastern Congo. Pearl's eventual rescue during the January 2002 eruption of *Nyirangongo* volcano near Goma was facilitated by *Kadogo*, a dog she raised and trained herself. O'Connor trained Army combat dogs in Georgia during the Vietnam War. He died long ago when his heart gave out on a cruel April morning.

Acknowledgments

Ondine & the Blue Troll, Saint Martin, Nzombi, The Flying Horse, Georges Dream, Old Mamadou, Sirèns, Regime of Bananas, Crazy Joseph, and Snakes & Violets were first published in "Ondine & the Blue Troll, Selected Short Stories (Rocket Science Press 2013). *Footnote to Doggerel* appeared in GREEN BLADE 2015 Edition, the former Magazine of the now defunct Rural America Writers' Center of Plainview, Minnesota. *Lily Jo* was first published in LOST LAKE FOLK OPERA V8 MAGAZINE, Autumn 2023, *Waterways* issue.

ABOUT THE AUTHOR

An Army veteran, returned Peace Corps Volunteer, and former design officer for the United States Agency for International Development, Tom Driscoll has a degree in English from the University of Iowa, and studied at the Iowa Playwrights Workshop. Author of fiction, poetry, plays, and journalism, including "Bleu: Selected Poems 1967 – 1998," and "Ondine & the Blue Troll," Tom is the Managing editor of Shipwreckt Books Publishing Company and Lost Lake Folk Opera literary magazine. He and his wife, Beth Stanford, live within spitting distance of the Mississippi River in Winona, Minnesota.

www.ingramcontent.com/pod-product-compliance
Lightning Source LLC
Chambersburg PA
CBHW030329020726
47493CB00004B/1211